# A SOLILOQUY OF SOME DISCONNECTED TALES

# A SOLILOQUY
## *of Some*
# DISCONNECTED TALES

*stories*

## THOMAS E. CHÁVEZ

Casa Urraca Press

ABIQUIÚ

Author photograph by Celia López-Chávez.
Set in Baskerville URW with touches of Baskerville.

First edition

28  27  26        2  3  4  5  6  7

ISBN 978-1-956375-39-8
Ebook ISBN 978-1-956375-28-2

CASA URRACA PRESS
an imprint of Casa Urraca, Ltd.
casaurracapress.com

Dedicated to the memory of my parents,
Marilyn Sprowl Chávez & Judge Antonio E. Chávez,
and to the future of my grandchildren,
Noé Antonio García Chávez &
Alexina Christel García Chávez.

# Contents

Dark swallow, you have returned
But not to her balconies.

To us, the most ephemeral of all,
Once each thing. No more. Nevermore.
And we, too, never again.

Do what we shall
We will forever be poised as one who departs.

Thus we live always: bidding farewell.

*–José Emilio Pacheco,*
*Mexican poet and essayist,*
*"Bécquer y Rilke se encuentran en Sevilla"*

*Introduction*

SOMETIME LATE IN THE SIXTEENTH CENTURY, Miguel de
Cervantes—no doubt with ink-stained hands and in a
state of euphoria for just having completed a novel many
years in the making—wrote:

> *Dear Reader: Without my swearing to it, you can
> believe that I would like this book, the child of my
> understanding, to be the most beautiful, the most
> brilliant, and the most discreet that anyone could
> imagine.*

He then went on to explain why that lofty ideal cannot
be met. So, I, a latter-day Quixote, as I have written
elsewhere, share the great barb's goal and reality.

I offer here a short book of interlocked stories and
streams of consciousness; a thought process not so linear
and even slightly disjointed. The book's concept began

not as an idea for a book or publication, but as an idea in my imagination that was inspired by a movie and a book about a centuries-old burial near the eastern shores of England that morphed into more stories, a majority of which, quite naturally, focus on New Mexico, the place where I was born and live. The stories are but a minuscule few and the resultant thought processes are as one planet in the universe. Yet, perhaps without shame, *sin vergüenza*, as is said in Spanish, I decided to put in book form these random stories interspersed with self-indulgent thoughts that are somewhat summed up by the Mexican poet José Emilio Pacheco's poem about the posthumous meeting of two other poets, Gustavo Adolfo Bécquer of Spain and Rainer Maria Rilke of Austria.

I hope that what little value this book brings will outweigh the ridicule it may invite. That said, I leave you, dear reader, with the words written by Samuel Johnson in 1753, which I used to start a different book I never published:

> *Shakespeare's Excellence is not the Fiction of a Tale, but the Representation of Life; and his Reputation is therefore safe, till Human Nature shall be changed.*

So, with a slightly edited version of Cervantes's words, I offer this narrative "the child of my limited understanding" and hope its damage to my reputation will be limited, at least, for a generation. "Till Human Nature shall be changed" might be too much to expect.

All of us, in our human and realized life,
are but the caricatures of our soul.

*—Fernando Pessoa,*
*Portuguese scholar and poet,*
*in a friend's autograph book, 1914*

## *Fate I*

THE MORNING LIGHT SEEPED through a window, providing respite. He lay there on the bed, his daughter crying, son looking sorrowful, and three grandchildren, all young adults, looking stoic but respectful. His life had ended. He is dead, just now expired—or so it seems.

"So, here we are. The time has come."

"Who are you?"

"Me? You. Your subconscious."

"Is this a dream?"

"Yes. Well, sort of. Only—if you are dead, when this dream ends, you will not awaken."

"What?"

"You—we—are dead."

"Sure. So, then we are talking in a dream ... dead?"

"I am a part of you. Waiting all these years for this moment. It is my only role in your—well, our—life. The last act, sort of."

There was no vision. The voice came out of the dark. Like a thought process but, like dreams, it seemed very real in the moment.

"Are you God? Is that what this is?"

"No. I am you. I told you. Everyone has this in themselves, and it only comes out at the moment—"

"Of death."

"Correct. Or close to it."

"And God. Is there a God?"

"I cannot speak to that. Who knows? Remember, I am you and you have your doubts. Wanting to believe. But, really, an agnostic. I guess we will have to find out together."

"How is that? If I am dead and talking to you."

"Yes, and that is it for me. I will die with you. After that, so far as I am concerned … nothing."

"So, I am not dead. I—" The voice cut him off.

"Your body has died. Your brain, where we live, has a few moments more. How can I say this? You know how people say that when a person dies, they can still hear you because their brain still functions, at least for a few more moments? Well, that is partially true. You can't hear anybody. We are the reality of that idea."

"But, will I be united with my loved ones who—"

"No. Not Mary Nordal, that beautiful lady who befriended you as a youth. Or your childhood buddy Manuel who died in Vietnam. Not even your parents or daughter. They will die with us in your memory."

"But—"

"Listen. Our time is short. We humans in all our myriad mysteries—physically and mentally, well, while alive we cannot solve the mystery of death. Nor, for that matter, the ancient mystery when the body unites with the cosmic soul. And here we are."

"But, our spirit. Surely there is something?"

"Maybe another mystery. To be taken in faith. If you want to believe that, who am I, your subconscious, to complain? Remember: there is the reality of memory. Your life's work, the books you wrote, some of your deeds … who knows what more. They will survive in the memories of those who continue to live as you maintained the memories of many people who died centuries ago. Your parents live in your mind—they still dictate your behavior, your moral compass. And you always spoke to your daughter. Did she talk back? Maybe. In your mind she did. Her spirit, their spirits, live in you, your memory, and your desire to honor them, to make them proud even after their deaths. That is my—our—definition of spirit. So, yes. There is something."

"Well, I guess that is it. A form of agnosticism. It is comforting in its own way."

"We are left to commiserate with ourselves. I—we—share a common lifetime with many, many memories. We lived a full, long life."

"Yes. So, this is what happens? The dead never hear all the accolades. The funeral oration? All that stuff? A culmination? Hopefully, a fitting end. A self-realization, then, if not an understanding, of death itself?"

"Yes, so it seems. There is one more thing—"

"What?"

"Acceptance."

"Yeah, maybe the most important—"

"—part of life. The certain end. But you knew that. I have known for the last few years."

"But you—"

"—said that I am aware to you only now. Yes? Yes. I lay dormant for most of your life, while time passes. Sometimes I sneak into your dreams. But when the time approaches, I am awakened to my function."

"You were forewarned."

"I am in your subconscious. Your physical deterioration, age, and the subsequent mentality conspired to waken me. Also, your increased disappointment of life itself. The acting-up replacement knee, the increased embarrassments, the forgetfulness. You even wet your pants once."

"Oh, that. I forgot."

"No, you didn't. Not in your subconscious. It added up. The frustration of knowing that your body could no longer do what it once did or what your mind still desired is a harbinger. It signaled your pending—shall we say—culmination."

"In other words, I—we—were, are ready."

"And in life you took it with grace. Everyone must die only with their conscience. That is my function."

"You have done it well."

"Our time is short, has come."

"And?"

"We will stop. Like a switch going off, only nothing. More than that, we know nothing."

"Unlike the song, time is not on our side. Thank you. Or should I thank me?"

"It is the same."

The house lightens up with the rising sun. The people from the morgue arrive and enter the bedroom. They wrap the body in the white sheets in which he lay, place him on the gurney, and wheel him out. That is the last his loved ones will see of him. He asked to be cremated.

# Irony
## *(Levigolde)*

IN THE FIRST PART OF THE SEVENTH CENTURY on the far eastern shore of what is today England, a small kingdom of Anglo-Saxons existed in a place that they called "Eastengia," or, in today's parlance, "East Anglia." In the year 624, the kingdom's most famous king, Raedwald, died. And according to his wishes, his heir and son buried him in a ship—for you see, Raedwald loved the sea.

Of course, Ecorpald, the new king, loved his father and went to great extremes to acquiesce to his father's wish. He even discussed with his helpers that the ship should not be one of the kingdom's bigger ones; rather, it should be one at once seaworthy, but in keeping with the rank of its perpetual inhabitant.

Ecorpald, still in mourning, called the people together, all of them subservient to him—many feared the new king as they had his father. A majority of the people were serfs, and their obedience was expected.

With his engineers they managed to transport a ship up the River Deben. They sailed part way from its mouth on the sea, then had to row, and, finally, push and pull the ship to as close as the chosen burial spot as they could get. The place was on a rise about a quarter of a mile from the river's bank.

There, Ecorpald gave orders to dig a pit deep enough to bury the ship and to be careful to leave a ramp in the direction of the river. With hundreds of laborers, the first two tasks of getting the ship upriver and preparing the burial pit had been completed. But there remained the last chore of transporting the boat over land to its final resting place. And this is where our story begins.

The new king stood on a rise, watching the progress of the ship moving ever so slowly. A multitude of serfs struggled as they placed logs under the front of the ship and rolled it forward. Five men grabbed the newly freed logs behind the ship and carried them to the ship's front to repeat the process. In this way, twenty men divided into five lines, labored as they picked up a freed log, carried it to the front where they placed it, then returned to the back of the line to wait for their turn to repeat the task. It was a slow, even tedious, process—but the method required consistency. That is to say: disturbances would not be tolerated among the men.

But, of course, humans being humans, on this particular day two disturbances occurred one after the other. The first involved a man who tried to slip back in line and thus avoid lifting the log. The others quite naturally objected, and a tussle broke out. The king's guards quickly separated the belligerents and learned the source of the problem, and he was taken before the king.

When told of the man's violation, the king ordered the man to face away from him as a guard with a razor-sharp knife cut across his back, leaving a bloody—but not deadly—wound.

"Now," said King Ecorpald, "you will be spotted among the many. Go to the front of the line."

Not long afterward, another episode of pushing and shoving broke out. With his patience tried, Ecorpald now faced the new instigator.

"Do you fear for your life? Do you not care for the burial of your king? What is so important that brings you here before me?"

The serf dropped to one knee. "Your Highness, I suppose it is because I am not liked by the others."

"Not liked? How does that matter?"

"It is because I dream of going to sea."

"Well, then. I can grant your wish. You will accompany my father on this ship."

The crestfallen serf bowed his head in obedience. He believed he had just received a death sentence.

But Ecorpald thought differently. "No, you are lucky. Such an act is not in our tradition. What is your name?"

"Levigolde, Your Highness."

"Levigolde, you will be confined to my royal court as a servant. For now, you will take your place in line."

Levigolde would go on to serve Ecorpald loyally and even go to sea. But we digress.

Levigolde came from a small—very small—coastal village that was not far—but far enough—from the kingdom's capitol. When Levigolde was a young boy of seven years old, the kingdom's mortal enemies came from the sea and sacked his village. The Vikings took pleasure in such activity. Levigolde saw them as large, hairy, ugly men who fed off the violence they created. Monsters.

By the luck of a wall that fell and buried Levigolde, who had taken refuge next to a hollowed-out water trough, he was able to survive the devastation. Lying there, he heard the screams, shouts, and, even, the victors' laughter as they rampaged through the unprotected village.

When they left, it became quiet—but the image remained in his mind of their ships approaching, along with the futile defense put up by the overmatched villagers. Levigolde had not even had a chance to say good-bye to his parents. He found his father lying grotesquely in the mud and blood, his mouth and eyes open as if astonished, and in one hand he held a hoe, his only weapon. His mother was never seen again.

Young Levigolde was found and taken to the capitol, where he was raised into a life of serfdom. But he never forgot his past and became fascinated with the king's small fleet of ocean-going ships.

So far as naval strength or expertise, the Eastengians were not a match for the Vikings. Their navy, such as it is, was for defense. The Vikings, for all their violence, preferred to attack the weak, the undefended. They avoided a force that presaged resistance. The Eastengians, good and feared warriors on land, had but a small defense on water. They were not real seafarers.

In the course of his young life, Levigolde worked in the shipyard mandated to any number of menial tasks. He helped carry wood to the shops. One time, he and fifteen or so other men carried a log that became the pole for a mast. But he always was observant and saw a path toward fulfilling a vow to find those who had killed his father and had taken his mother. And the others became tired of his constant rambling on about going to sea to confront the Vikings—a name that, incidentally, he never used for them. He chose derogatory names instead. Everyone knew who he meant.

Thus, now, as he worked among the lines moving the burial ship, some of the men became inpatient with his prattling about the sea. The ensuing disturbance caught the king's attention, leading to Levigolde's sentence.

Maybe Escorpald saw something of value in Levigolde. Whatever the reason, Levigolde soon won the king's favor and moved up in ranks. If he so desired to confront Vikings, why not put him in the military? Moreover, as he proved himself there, the king granted his wish to assign him to one of the ships defending the port. With that, Levigolde's desire to go to the sea had become partially fulfilled. He had yet to actually confront a Viking. (He did not count the few border skirmishes in which he had participated against neighboring kingdoms.)

Nevertheless, with the king's favor, he continued to move up in ranks, eventually to be put in charge of one of the ships. And the day came when he spotted a Viking ship cruising off the coast to, perhaps, in his mind, look for a village to plunder. And he would not let that happen—never—on his watch.

It was late afternoon and the sun had begun to drop when the Vikings changed direction to head out to sea. Usually at such moments, the Eastengians happily, if not with some relief, would watch it drop below the horizon. But Levigolde had a different idea. With the sun at his back, he ordered his ship to the east, in pursuit of the other ship.

His men were astounded at the order, so he explained: "For once we will take it against them. I see your concern. The sun is behind us and thus we are obscured to the dogs. They are blinded looking into its brilliance. Also, they will not look because they think us cowards and would never attack them. Well, this time they will be surprised. And, yes, after sundown, the dark of the night, the small moon will keep our surprise."

The surprise was complete. They caught the Vikings, who had not reacted quickly enough to prevent their capture.

Reflecting the confidence of the moment, Levigolde led his men when they jumped onboard the enemy ship. The battle lasted a few minutes before the Vikings dropped their weapons among the bodies strewn around them.

Levigolde had won his revenge. But he was not through. He ordered that the two ships exchange sails so that his would be identified as a Viking ship. Then, he took the water and food from the captured ship as well as the few slaves they had in turn captured from who knows where. Thus, stripped of supplies and with an Eastengian sail, the Vikings were set loose. Levigolde knew that they would seek the closest and safest port, if not by then getting attacked by one of their own.

Still not satisfied and taking advantage of being on the high seas, Levigolde decided to take a prolonged return route, hoping to spot another Viking ship—which, he indeed did. This time the newly installed Viking sail provided the surprise Levigold had hoped for. Once again, they won a quick victory. And this time, Levigolde took the defeated crew prisoner, divided his own crew, and took his prize back to Eastengia where, understandably, he became an instant hero and admired by none more so than King Escorpald.

Although he never again captured a Viking ship, he led a successful career defending the kingdom's port and small coastal villages. And although he would never know, his reputation spread among the Vikings, who preferred to avoid him or a ship that they thought might be his. These victories led to a period of peace while Levigolde's stature grew over time.

But then came the day when Escorpald fell ill and was put to bed. Expecting death, he called for Levigolde to be at his side. Upon seeing his trusted warrior, the king reached out a hand. Levigolde held it affectionately as the king spoke.

"Ah, Levigolde, how I remember those many years ago when you told me of your desire. And you went to sea, met the cursed Vikings. Did you not?"

"Yes, sire. Because of you."

"And you remember you were allowed to fulfill this desire rather than accompany my father?"

"It is so, sire."

"Yes. So now, will you be my death's guide? My protector?" Escorpald, becoming increasingly weak, coughed.

Levigolde did not hesitate. "As you desire, My Lord."

"Yes, I expected that answer. You have accomplished enough in this life and now must begin anew with me in the next life."

"Yes."

"You are honorable. Always have been. Your life is the sea and mine is the land. I will not be buried as my father was, but in a crypt. Nor has it become customary to bury a companion. No, you have earned your own destiny. Live it well as I know you will."

Somewhat overcome with his king's words, an emotional Levigolde replied, "Sire, I will live in your spirit. All that I will do will be done to win your approbation."

Escorpald died a few days later, and for the next fourteen years Levigolde did indeed continue to live an honorable life—at the end of which he suffered a natural death. Little did he know that during those earlier years, King Escorpald left instructions as to how Levigolde's final resting place should be handled: his body—laid out on a flat, draped bed—was carried to a river bank where long ago he had helped take Raedwald's ship to be buried. There, Levigolde was laid on top of a small, specially made boat and escorted downriver to the open sea, where his pall bearers loosened a small sail and left the wind and water to carry him off while the populace watched his body float toward the horizon until he could be seen no longer.

# *Fate II*

I AM DEAD, or, at least—

Wait!

Then, another voice: "Talking to me, I presume?"

"No, I was—"

"I know, talking to or with your subconscious. Its work is done. Like your physical self, it is dead. Gone."

"—still here. And now? You?"

"Your spirit."

"My spirit?"

"Yes."

"A spirit. Does this have something to do with soul or God? Does God exist?"

"In a sense, yes. I am you, and you are me. Together we shall live beyond your death. The spirit lives in different modes. It can morph into different entities. There is the spirit of your memory or, to be clear, the memory of you that others have—others, like your family, loved ones, close friends. This memory varies depending on the people you touched emotionally, intellectually, spiritually. This spirit can be good or bad."

The voice continues, "Then there is the spirit of your actions. You, for example, wrote. Published books and articles. Those who read them will imbibe in your spirit. The same for your letters and some of your photographs, the things that you supported and the ideas you had that came or will come into fruition."

"Will come?"

"I cannot predict the future, nor plan it. Did you not finish a biography of another who passed away? Yes, in doing so, you moved his memory forward, incorporated his spirit."

'Then there is the spirit of the intangible. That of your being, your personality, that has had a lasting effect and could survive generations.

So, you see? That is how an excavation not only revised the memory of a long-buried king, but it also conjured up the memory of those who struggled to bury him."

"Lest I forget. At times we will join the spirits of others. You would call it 'influence.' Others, I think 'osmosis.' An unseen type of cross-pollination is closer to the truth. And this journey can be positive or negative."

He could not believe he was hearing voices, but he supposed he must be dead. He rubbed his eyes and decided to engage the voice.

"Again, we come to good and bad, yin and yang. Must it be so simple?"

"Normally no. That is a determination made in its time and the result of its act. But there is no judgment. It is what it is, or was at the time. I, your spirit, was long ago deeply joined to that of your wife. In that sense she is you and you her. And when the time comes, she will learn the same. Actually, when people hear the voices of loved ones who have passed—"

"That is their spirit, memory coming from the mind?"

"Yes."

## Myth and Reality
## (Joan of Arc, Cervantes, and Juana la Loca)

THEN THE SPIRIT, like the subconscious seemingly disconnected, started speaking of a subject not thought about for a long time.

"If anything, people have heard of Joan of Arc. They assume that she is a saint of some kind, a woman, and a knight, a soldier. Others, especially in France, are more aware of her as the savior of France.

"You know the story. She died young, never got out of her teenage years. She had exceptional strength and ability with the arms of the day. She claimed to be the fulfillment of a French legend that France would be destroyed by a woman and restored by a virgin. No matter whether she knew it, the basis of this legend came from the visions of a soothsayer named Marie Robine of Avignon. Joan played on this idea, and with what must have been an exceptional charisma, she captured the ear of the Dauphin, the future King Charles VII of France.

"As a young lady, sixteen or seventeen years old, she ended up in the front lines opposing the English occupation of France. Her prowess included pulling an arrow out of her lower neck and shoulder, rising from a fall off of a siege ladder after being hit by a stone, and always joining the engagement at its most dangerous point. She always sought to attack, to advance. Because she survived and succeeded, the troops rallied around her. She became an inspirational leader. In her presence, the heretofore depressed Armagnac armies loyal to the Dauphin starting winning victories. She helped lift the siege of Orléans, encouraged and participated in the Loire Campaign that resulted in a victory at Patay, and, then, encouraged and led the French army in taking Reims unopposed, so Charles could be crowned the King of France.

"She had become a legend in her day. But that status was a double-edged sword. Because of her, Charles VII was the recognized king. Yet, despite having her at his side during the coronation, he became jealous of her. He saw her as a political liability. Her accomplishments reflected on his inability to do the same. And, she was a woman.

"As a result, he let her continue to go to battle, but with less support of men and armaments. Finally, while engaging the enemy with a small contingent of her own men, she was captured. Contrary the custom of the time, Charles never offered a ransom for her release. His silence resonated for its intent. And the British fulfilled his desire when in London she was tried and sentenced, and they lit her pyre. The year was 1431 and she was nineteen years old.

"Within a lifetime of her death, the Catholic Church condemned their very own officials who had presided over her trial and execution. The Church declared her a saint.

"What about today? Well, you know that answer. She is remembered, even venerated, and who can name that French Dauphin who became the king because of her exploits? No one. Charles VII lived a full life and even played a key role in finally ending the One Hundred Years' War. Still, she is remembered and he—well, he was another king.

"So, you see, here is a story where legend, myth, and fact come together in a real person who truly accomplished what appear to be other-worldly acts. Almost two centuries later, Miguel Cervantes wrote about his fictional Don Quixote, exclaiming that his protagonist would become so famous 'that death itself did not triumph over his life.'"

He stopped the spirit. "Wait! How can you remember that?"

"I? No, you!"

"Me?"

"I am you, like your subconscious. I have access to things, memories that you think are forgotten. Yet they linger and, in their own way, can surface when inspired."

He smiled at the thought of some humorous anecdote. "So, I am smarter than I think."

Silence followed for an uneasy moment. Then: "Let us get back to the story. So, today or, even, a lifetime after Cervantes's death, who can name the king or kings that ruled Spain during his life? As with Joan of Arc, no one! Joan became one of the most famous heroines in history as well as the patron saint of France. Like Joan of Arc, Don Quixote and his creator Miguel de Cervantes have outlived their respective kings in common thought."

He attempted to correct the spirit: "But Felipe II, I know, was Cervantes's king for most of his life. He is well-known. Books have been written about him. And Quixote? He is a fictional character!"

"Yes, true—yet, if a common person is asked who ruled Spain when Cervantes wrote, the answer would be a guess at best. Even in Spain."

Now enthused, he spoke up: "Even today our politicians are buried with headlines, but writers, creative minds, less so. Your diatribe about Joan of Arc reminds me of another of yesteryear's women: Juana la Loca, the daughter of Fernando and Isabel, the fourteenth century king and queen who unified Spain by marriage and conquest.

"Juana and her husband inherited the throne. Because of politics led by both her husband and father, and then her husband's sudden and suspicious death, she fell into what today would be called clinical depression. The fact, that, in her grief, she held off burying her husband was reason enough for the men of her regime, to proclaim her mad, and they placed her under house arrest in a fortified palace in Todesillas, Spain. She would never be released, as even her son—who became Carlos I of Spain and Carlos V as the Holy Roman Empire—ignored her.

She died at seventy-five years of age, forty-eight years of which were spent under lock and key.

"In fulfillment to the wishes of Juana's mother, Queen Isabela, in 1517, the remains of Juana, Felipe, Fernando, and Isabel, sealed iron caskets were placed in a crypt below two ornate sculptures in a specially built royal chapel annexed to Granada's cathedral. The sculptures have an interesting feature: Juana and Felipe are shown in death lying on ornate beds with their heads resting on three large pillows. The same is true for Fernando and Isabel. Domenico Facelli oversaw these works of art. He apparently had doubts about the story of Juana's insanity. Three of the four pillows are indented under the weight of the heads resting on them. The exception is the pillow under Felipe's head. There is no indention in his pillow. Did the artist do this because it was Felipe who had the empty head?

Despite Facelli's ploy, Juana's legacy as a woman who lost her wits has survived through the ages. That is, until today. Now, finally, historians have questioned whether Juana's insanity was real—or was it a ploy to have her removed by men who desired power that was rightfully hers? While locked up, she wrote letters that indicate her sanity, confirm the documented brilliance of her youth, and call into question her centuries-long sobriquet."

# *Fate III*

As if regaining a consciousness, he looked around and saw nothing. Darkness did not exist. Instead, a translucent light prevailed. For some reason the thought came to him that this must be what it looks like inside a ping pong ball. *What? Where did that come from?*

And then, a familiar voice answered: "From a description that a pilot once told you about flying in what he called 'weather.'"

He recognized the voice of his conscience. "We are not through."

"No."

"Am I dead or not?"

"Actually, I am not sure. This is unusual."

"Unusual? What do you mean?"

"This is prolonged. I have no answer."

"Answer? From whom or what? Death is definite … I should think."

"Do you believe that?"

"I don't know—but yes, I guess. I know it is not like some books written for the grieving where they use the example of a caterpillar that morphs into a butterfly."

"You don't believe that?"

"The butterfly dies. What then?"

"And you are the butterfly."

"In a manner of speaking, yes."

"You once copied a statement about death from a Roman burial stone that you saw in a museum: 'Life—'"

"'—is the target of envy.' From the second century. I remember."

"Then you copied another line from somewhere. Shall I repeat it?"

"Yes."

"'Death, the final outcome. Only ideological imagery or hope could lend it meaning.'"

"Those words came from an eighteenth-century man who I was researching. In the end, he credited the will of God to his suffering and pending death. That reminds me of another citation that I copied from a Canopic jar that contained the remains of a bull, which was considered sacred in Egypt." He scurried through his notes, not noticing that the search was in his mind and not physically done. "Here, here it is: 'Night is born of sleep and death.'"

"Why do you remember those words?"

The question brought him back to the reality of his presence. He did not look for the phrase but remembered it. As to the question, he only could answer the truth.

"Because I never could understand what they meant. They appear to be profound, but their significance is lost on me. Obviously, night begins and ends with day."

"Maybe that is the reason we have been extended. There are some questions that need answers."

## *Persistence*
## *(Sylvester Sprowl)*

ALLEN HAD DONE HIS RESEARCH. Now with his car parked, he walked on an especially manicured green lawn. He didn't notice the baby blue sky, bright sunlight, or many fully-leafed trees. Nor did he care to notice any clouds. He continued through the measured, identifiable headstones. He was about to close a circle begun a century and a half earlier.

His own part of the story had begun on a cul-de-sac in Southern California when, as a young man in his twenties, he had stood there with his elderly father and his two teenage nephews. As if it were a matter of fact, Allen's father stated, "My uncle was a hero in the Civil War."

The looks of disbelief on their faces characterized an unconvinced audience. This was the 1960s. The Civil War took place a hundred years before. The old man must be telling a tale, they thought, but he continued: "He fought for the north."

The younger of the two grandsons made a snide remark that Allen did not appreciate. He punched the kid's arm with a blow meant to be felt.

None of the three in his audience realized it then, but the old man's words had resonated with them. One of the grandsons (he who had snickered) became a historian. Years later he and Allen brought up the subject. Could it be true? Allen embarked on a genealogical journey of his own family.

And that journey had brought him now to the hallowed grounds of a national cemetery containing the burials of fallen Civil War soldiers. Wax poetic, sing praises, or merely look: no matter. When a person is from the Southwest, no matter how well-travelled, that person is used to skies so clear that the blue changes color and clouds so white that a person needs to squint to look at them. Used to open landscapes that stretch forever, where mountains and buttes tincture the expansive spaces—where they even peek from behind the horizon as mysterious grayish-blue masses. Among such landmarks and sacred places, a person senses how minuscule humans really are in the great cosmos.

Naturally, the mountainous, fully vegetated terrain of Tennessee intrigued and awed Allen as he walked through the site. So much greenery, so much moisture, and so different from home. He had long since moved to New Mexico. Then there was the humidity, which draped him like an electronically heated jacket. Sweaty, he looked for the headstone of a heretofore-unknown relative: a young man from Ohio whose permanent residence, if you want to call it that, is Chattanooga, Tennessee. If he knew what Allen was doing, he would be surprised because no one in the family had visited him since he left the farm.

He had read far too many names and dates, but he immediately forgot all that. *Here it is!* The white, upright, manicured stone with the name *Sylvester Sprowl, Corporal* and the dates 1843–1863.

Ah, yes, the farm. Sylvester Sprowl, the third of nine children born between 1839 and 1859, had not especially enjoyed the farm and left when his youngest brother, Franklin, was still a toddler of three years old. That was the last time he saw him.

And that takes us back to 1860 and a fifty-nine-acre farm with a nice, new, two-story house outside of Salem, Ohio. Franklin, of course, would never remember Sylvester—although, as he grew up, he would hear of him often, for Sylvester became somewhat of a distant legend. The immediate family would tell stories of Sylvester, who was born on the farm sixteen years before Franklin. His oldest brother, Martin, was his senior by four years and the next oldest sibling, George, was two years his junior. But we digress.


Seventeen-year-old Sylvester Sprowl is hunched over, carefully walking as he spots a nice, plump pheasant. The bird freezes; Sylvester stops. He is experienced enough to know that if he does not take a shot now, he will lose the opportunity.

He raises the family's old percussion cap Hawkins rifle, holds his breath, aims at the brightly colored green, red, white, and gray bird, and fires. The gun's hammer snaps, the powder ignites, and the gun recoils as the lead ball is propelled toward its target. He misses. In a flurry of flapping wings, feathers, sticks, and leaves, the pheasant flees from his near-death experience.

Sylvester lowers his rifle and stares at the scene. He has lost the opportunity to take home a nice dinner. The missed shot will cost the family in two ways. He has wasted a lead ball. Lead costs precious money or trade. And the loss of meat means that they will have to replace it with a couple of their own chickens—if not that night, then another.

Sylvester has enough years on him to know that survival means attention to detail, and that means work. At first "pitching in," he is now an invaluable cog in the family's struggle for self-sufficiency. Like in most families of the day, Sylvester and his siblings had been given chores as soon as they were old enough to understand what to do. Survival was paramount. The majority of their time and thought went into extracting a living from the farm— and the more hands, the better. Maybe, just maybe, their labor combined with favorable weather could produce a slight excess that could be sold or traded at the village market.

◊ ◊ ◊

For all of his life, most of which did not qualify as adulthood, Sylvester shared chores—work, really—with Martin and George. They rarely missed sunrise and returned to the house at sunset only because they could not work in the dark, and lighting the barn risked burning the whole structure down. The women fixed dinner, after which the family talked, played cards, or just sat and day-dreamed before going to bed early enough to rise well before dawn the next day.

They lived a little over four miles from the village of Salem, a little further from the smaller hamlet of Canfield. Salem consisted of one street, a store, a stable, a bar, and restaurant. A small, two-story boarding house and veterinarian's office defined the beginning of a side street. The animal doctor sometimes expanded his clientele to humans.

Whether Sylvester knew it or not, life had become repetitious and boring. It was tranquil. And then the startling news spread through the farming community that seven states had seceded from the union, formed an army, and had fired upon Fort Sumter in South Carolina. This was nothing less than an outright rebellion.

Abraham Lincoln, the newly elected President of the United States—who, every mid-westerner knew, was one of them because he grew up in Indiana and Illinois—issued a call for troops to quell the rebellion. Recruiting stations opened throughout Ohio, and the one in Alliance, a mere fifteen miles away, beckoned. Sylvester, with a youth's enthusiasm for adventure—if not a romantic idea of war—announced to his family that he was joining up.

He and all the other farm boys like him could not help but be impressed. They had new, blue uniforms, regular meals, and were handed newly minted smoothbore rifles. Sylvester's enthusiasm did not wane during training. *This*, he thought, *is easier than farm work*. And, as he looked around at all the soldiers in their uniforms, he was sure they were invincible. Why would anyone dare to oppose such a force?

If he had any doubts, the news of the Confederate victory at Manassas came as a shock. The boys talked among themselves.

"How many were killed?" someone asked.

Another answered, "I heard 'round three thousand."

It hardly seemed cleaning their guns mattered as they talked.

"On our side?"

"Yep."

"What 'bout the rebs?" (That was what they called the rebels.)

"They won the battle."

"Okay. But what 'bout their dead?"

Someone else joined in: "What does it matter? Maybe two thous."

Another chimed in: "Where's Manassas?"

This question elicited displeased grunts because none of the boys had an answer.

Initially, Sylvester's regiment, the 19th of Company 1 of the Ohio Infantry, marched to different places but did not engage the enemy. Sylvester and his companions did not know what a Confederate soldier looked like. They heard that they wore gray uniforms but not much else. Oh, and the officers warned them that the "rebs" liked to yell and scream to scare them: "So be ready."

At first, marching was painful because of their newly issued shoes. They marched and rode trains to places Sylvester had never heard of—well, maybe Louisville but not Lebanon, Renick's Creek, Jamestown, Greasy Creek—and, finally, through Nashville south to Savannah, Tennessee. They had walked almost four months and no one had become a hero.

Then, they were told their chances to be heroes would be imminent: "Get ready to move out."

"We gonna hear 'em scream and yell first?"

Sylvester didn't talk much. He had never seen a dead man, or, at least, one who died from something other than old age, like his step-grandfather.

"Shit," Sylvester said. "Never heard a scream could stop a well-aimed ball." He fondled his rifle as the others nodded or mouthed their agreement. "Should be easier pickings than pheasant."

A new constant sound in the distance disturbed his thoughts. It sounded like thunder that was speckled—the only word he could think of—with rifle shots. And he could see, as they formed up, that the officers had pointed the contingent toward the source of that sound.

No sleep. No sleep, and Sylvester did not notice. The sudden rush of orders and movement, a rapid forced march, and then boarding the ferry to cross the river—he did not know the name—then positioned for an attack or, worse, to defend against the enemy's advance. He had never seen so many men. Not in any town or even the local fairs had he seen so many people gathered. He didn't know the number, but he easily could see that his side had thousands—if not tens of thousands—of men.

*What,* he wondered, *are we going to face if we need a force this big?*

Reality had begun to sink in. Time became seamless.

Then, it rained—a major thunderstorm that would not stop. He had become used to inclement weather, mud, then mosquitos. This particular storm seemed a harbinger of what dawn would bring. All that he could think was to keep his ammunition dry.

But then, he noticed something different. More men had moved in around him. These were not the boys he had come with. These men looked worn, lost. Some had rifles; others didn't. He could not tell for sure, but some appeared to be bleeding or were hurt. This wasn't a dream. Through the driving rain and water running down his face, the men appeared as illusions moving slowly and with blank faces. Then, he knew: they were the remnants of the day's fighting. The survivors.

The rain stopped. Word came: "We are in silent mode. No fires."

*Who could light one anyway? Everything is drenched. They must be close. What's that?*

His mind raced, but the last question came out of his mouth. It sounded like a moan—no, moans, someone crying, begging for help.

"What?" he repeated.

One of the recent arrivals saw the question in Sylvester's face, whether he actually heard him can be left to conjecture. He whispered an answer: "The wounded."

"Wounded?"

"From today—rather, yesterday. The field is full with the dead and dying."

Then the order came: "Forward."

*In the dark?*

Sylvester moved. He could barely see the forest across the open field. Lumps—bodies—barely became visible. Sylvester almost tripped over one, then something grabbed his pant leg. Sylvester looked down to a pained, bearded face.

"Help me," it said.

Sylvester pulled his leg free and kept moving further into the open.

*Thank God,* he thought, *for the cover of the night's darkness.* Not even the moon showed it face, having sunk behind the distant horizon and trees.

The rapid cracks, not booms, of the artillery behind him woke him from his thoughts. Then the ever-closer trees lit up whenever one of the cannonballs hit. Every so often, he thought he could see the silhouette of a man. Then, he had no doubt: men, screaming and yelling, rushed out of the trees, charging at them. The pheasant, his targets. But he never hunted the bird in the dark and pheasants never charged.

*Crack!*

Then, a multitude of cracks all rolled into one, and he thought: *Pheasants don't shoot back!*

Some of the men on either side of Sylvester returned fire, but to no avail. They were beyond range. The officers madly tried to stop them.

"Wait until they are in range. Wait for the order."

A kind of calm came over Sylvester. He seemed to be outside of himself.

*So, this is war. I am in a battle.*

A sense of change came over him. He had heard somewhere that boys go to war and come back men. He wondered when that happened.

His rifle already primed and raised, he heard the order to fire. He fired.

He did not miss. Nor did he feel euphoric. But, then, he had no time to feel anything but to reload and fire again. Sylvester's line held, and the Confederate attack was repulsed. They kept marching over bodies, in mud, through wet grass.

And then: another Confederate charge. They knelt or laid behind any protection they could find and fired some more. Later on, Sylvester would recall hearing the enemy's bullets snapping leaves or grass around him and hearing the whizzing of cannon balls traveling through the night in either direction.

He hardly noticed men falling. He kept moving forward when the order came. The second attack had also been repulsed.

Now, they came to the tree line. Finally, better protection. They moved forward from tree to fallen tree, around bushes. The sun had risen at the horizon, and Sylvester thanked the orb for its light. He could see his game, sort of. And they could see him.

They fired at each other, thousands of men. The artillery continued to pound the land, sometimes finding its mark, leaving body parts in its wake. Men fell; others replaced them. Sylvester remained untouched. *This is war.* He was numb to the destruction around him; he felt invincible yet not. He knew the next bullet could find him.

The smoke from thousands of percussion weapons and explosions once again obscured visibility. Now conscious of the immediate world around him, he moved more consciously, very selectively firing at movement in front of him. Time passed and the sun had risen, the heat pounded down but he did not notice either. He had been fighting over eight hours, and, just past mid-day, an uncommon silence came over the devastation. The enemy had left the field. Be cautious though. Wait to hear something officially. Still, no one returned fire. Slowly as the men realized they were firing at nothing, maybe as the smoke rose and they could see, they stopped shooting and looked around at each other, wondering what would be next.

But it was a false peace. The gray-coats fell back to regroup and charged again. This time the vegetation worked in Sylvester's favor. The rebels could not penetrate the Union lines. They tried more than once—and, after a slight lull, the order came to move forward. Sylvester heard a line officer yell back, "We have them on the run!"

That battle was won!

An exhausted, hungry, and mentally numb Sylvester joined his comrades in the night's bivouac, thankful for a chance to rest. Time would come later when they would think more clearly about what they had been through.

War has no concern about fatigue, or so it seemed.

Within an hour, Sylvester's unit was ordered to scout the enemy's assumed position to determine if they, in fact, had retreated and were regrouping. With scouts in front and to the sides, they marched on a road, which seemed pleasurable given the dead bodies populating the spaces beyond it. They hardly noticed the persistent mud. Nor did they care much about anything except their own pains and exhaustion.

One man grumbled about marching again, and the others within earshot made gestures of agreement. Then another spoke up: "Rather do this than gather the dead."

A hesitant silence followed until someone else asked, "Rebs too?"

Ignoring the question, the first person continued with his own thoughts: "The smell and flies. Actually, touching them."

He spit to emphasize the point.

"What do they do with them?"

"The rebs or ours?"

"Either, I guess."

"Don't know. Bury them?"

They stopped. The enemy had been sighted: about eight hundred of them left to guard and dismantle a field hospital. The rebels had cut trees and laid them out to impede an all-out attack. It worked.

Sylvester and his fellow soldiers had picked their way through the trunks and branches. Then, they came under fire. They slowly advanced using the foliage to their advantage. It seemed the Rebels had achieved what they intended: to buy time—so they could gather themselves, the patients, and whatever equipment was left and flee on wagons, horses, and on foot. Sylvester could see a wagon begin to move, but the soldiers remained in place, maintaining a constant fire. For the first time, he actually could pause and look at his adversaries. He noticed that they were not as well-armed as the Union troops. They had all sorts of weapons ranging from shotguns to old flintlocks to pistols. Now he realized that the enemy was with inferior arms and outnumbered. Still, they put up a stubborn defense.

They slowly advanced, pausing only to return fire. Sylvester wondered why they kept fighting. *They would lose. What value is the hospital to them?*

But—*what?* Sylvester could not believe it. The Rebs were charging just as the Union forces began to clear the last of the fallen trees. Now, with their traditional yells, they ran toward the superior Union force. The surprise was effective to a degree. A few men alongside Sylvester fell as they scrambled back into cover of the trees. Then, it became a slaughter. Shooting pheasant had not been this easy.

Even a farm boy like Sylvester wondered at the logic of the Rebels' moves as he watched the remnants of the grey-uniformed men retreat. They fled past the hospital, leaving it and a field strewn with bodies.

This time, Sylvester and his victorious fellows had the duty to "clean up," which meant turning their attention to that field.

First, they identified the wounded and took them to the abandoned hospital that had been set up anew. It was nothing more than a large tent with a few cots.

Then, they had to gather the dead. They laid the bodies in lines with the Union and Confederate men separated. The next task repulsed Sylvester. They had to search each corpse for its identification and for a possible last letter written "just in case."

The illiterate, like Sylvester, could have someone write the letter for them. An underground business of last-letter scribes had developed during the war, and they put their skills to good use. Sylvester, however, had chosen not to pay for such a service. Frugality had been pounded into him his whole life. He would simply have to survive.

And he had survived two engagements within the last forty-eight hours. He had become a veteran. Now he knew war, and it was anything but romantic. Nor would it wait.

After a month of confrontations and heavy artillery barrages against the Confederates—who had set up trenches and pickets outside Corinth, a railroad crossroads in northern Mississippi—they forced the town's evacuation.

At this point, Sylvester and his fellow Union soldiers had no doubt: they were deep in Confederate territory.

They had no idea what the overall strategy was. They just knew they had accomplished *something*. They were alive, had survived, and felt victorious as they pursued the retreating Rebels into northern Alabama and back to middle Tennessee.

In Savannah, they were given a small respite before orders arrived to march back to Nashville and, from there, to go north. Sylvester immediately recognized that they were retracing their route. They even used the same roads and were relieved to be on the same train that had brought them partway south. He wondered why they headed north? Is this a retreat? He didn't understand.

Word came down that they would pursue a Confederate force in Kentucky, a state that had become important in what the officials in Washington started calling the Western Campaign. No one explained how the enemy had gotten into Kentucky. After all, Kentucky had been secured. Now, they had to return to fight for lost ground. Such an image can easily demoralize a soldier, and Sylvester was no exception.

It took more than a month of marching before Louisville came into view. Those early battles had become a distant memory. They heard that the press had called the first battle "Shiloh." The newspapers claimed that it was the bloodiest battle of the war so far, with an estimated four thousand deaths and almost twenty thousand total casualties. The only answer to that news among the men was "*Shiiiiitttt*," then silence. Each left with their own thoughts about how or why they survived.

Soldiering gave them a lot of time to think, let their minds wander. That is the way of war: a lot of time to yourself, then a flash of (usually intense) violence.

"Pursuit" did not exactly apply for what they were doing. "Maneuvering" or "positioning" and waiting for the advantage to confront the Confederate force would be more appropriate. The two armies, like cocks in a pit, moved, eyed each other, and looked for the opportunity to engage. In this case, fate met reality, for the two forces would meet. Where and when would be the only question.

The beauty of Kentucky gave way to thoughts of a pending battle. Like everyone around him, Sylvester kept his rifle clean. Everything else about him reeked with filth. There was little time for personal hygiene. He had one uniform. His knapsack contained extra socks and a pair of shorts and undershirt. He tried to change once a week, but if not given time by a water source, nothing—including himself—could be cleaned. He used his knife and lice comb, items he brought from the farm, to keep his hair and growing beard under a semblance of control. Aside from some rest and maybe some cooked food, the bivouacs helped little when it came to hygiene.

The battle at Perryville took place on October 7 and 8, five months after Corinth and six months after Shiloh. Sylvester's company suffered the brunt of the Confederate attack. A storm of metal and lead raked the ranks. The battle would later be described as "thunder in the trees." They retreated to a stone wall, where what was left of them stalled the Confederate advance until they disengaged. He had become used to the destruction and death. He was numb to the bodies, whole or not, falling around him. Except for some scratches and small cuts, he survived another battle.

They occupied the small village, then were called again to "clean up." Sylvester's distaste for this duty surpassed his fear of war. Given no choice, he did his duty, filling a knapsack with the identifications of dead soldiers. He delivered the tags to a sergeant seated at a table inside a tent's entrance. Sylvester noticed his captain working at a separate table, on which he had writing materials and a stack of identifications.

Captain Sam'l Firestone knew Sylvester well. They each had survived the same conflicts and there were very few like them left. Sylvester did not feel out of place asking the captain what he was doing.

Firestone put down his pen and, with folded ink-stained hands, answered, "Letters. Letters to the families of our dead."

"Oh."

Sylvester had no other words. He turned and left, after which he remembered that he forgot to salute. He hoped that such a letter would not be written for him.

Then, he wondered, *And what if the captain was killed? Who would write his letter?*

The officers were dying as fast as the men in the lower ranks. Sylvester decided that he should give up some tobacco to send a letter home to let his parents know that he was alive. At this point, he had been away for more than a year.

After Perryville, Sylvester spent the next year being transported on trains or marching, camping, and engaging in small skirmishes, except for the fight at Stone's River. In the process, by reason of his survival, he was promoted to corporal. Finally, he and his unit went through the Cumberland Gap and stopped in a semi-wooded, hilly place called Chickamauga.

Chickamauga was a major battle won by the Confederates. For once, Sylvester's unit was not in the forefront, but it did not matter. Two great masses of men faced each other, opened fire, and began moving forward toward each other. The collapse of the Union's right flank left Sylvester's unit severely exposed. The retreating men panicked, and the enemy's quick advance at their flank made no sense to Sylvester. His instinct dictated that he stand and fight as he had done before.

Something otherworldly came over him. He had volunteered to be the standard bearer for his company when the previous bearer, a sergeant, had fallen in the previous day's skirmish. Holding the Stars and Stripes upright, he beseeched his fellow soldiers to rally with him. Then—

He felt it. *Oh, the burn.*

*I don't feel good. I have never felt this way. No. The blood. It's fresh. Is that mine? I'm losing my breadth. Where is it coming from? Hang on—the pole, the flag. Hold it tighter. Oh God, so weak. What's wrong? Rest. I can sit here just for a moment. No one cares. I need to rest to get some strength, to get ... out ... of ... here.*

The hunter had become the hunted. He was left for dead, shot through the chest as initially reported by Captain Firestone, who wrote a subsequent letter to "Benedict Sprowl and family" on October 10, 1863, some twenty days after Sylvester's supposed death. As he had done numerous times, Captain Firestone began the letter with, "It is my painful duty to announce the fate of your son." Then, he explained that Sylvester had been wounded, left for dead, and found to be alive by the Confederates, who took him to their field hospital where, days later, he died. He assured the family that Sylvester died heroically:

> *His position was a dangerous one. The Color Bearer is aimed at by the foe more than any other. Yet he feared not, faltered not. He bore the "Stars and Stripes" aloft for all. He fell mortally wounded, and the stain of this noble boy's blood is still upon the Flag Staff. I saw him last on Sunday noon. The Regiment had been routed and was streaming to the rear in utter confusion. Sylvester kept his post, and when all, all had left him. I saw him standing in the middle of the iron hail still waving his flag and distinctly heard him call to his retreating comrades to "rally round the Flag." He was known as one of the brave [... who] has fallen. Great God! What a cruel, cruel war.*

Captain Firestone signed off, put down his pen, and sat in silence. He had come to know Sylvester. He would be missed. But, then again, Sylvester's letter would not be the last such letter he would write.

A copy of that letter survived in the National Archives well over a century, when Allen Sprowl, following up on his dad's claim that the family included a Civil War hero, found it.

A little more research led Allen to the records of Sylvester's regiment. Left with nothing more to find, Allen, Sylvester Sprowl's grandnephew, determined that he would find his ancestor's grave, if it existed.

He used the excuse of a family vacation in the Florida panhandle to rent a car and drive north by himself in search of the grave. He went first to the Chickamauga and Chattanooga Battlefields, now well-manicured National Parks, the latter of which is a National Cemetery. And, after an inquiry and short search, Allen found his ancestor's grave: location site 234, section A in the Chattanooga National Cemetery on the site of the subsequent battle that resulted in a major Union victory.

Allen stared at the white marker with Sylvester's name, then set the timer on his camera and took a photograph of himself squatting next to it. He became the first and only family member to visit and pay his respects to Sylvester Sprowl, fulfilling the spirit of his father and great-uncle.

## *Fate IV*

THE SPIRIT SPOKE: "By now you understand that Sylvester lost his youth, then his life. Your ancestor fought in major and very bloody battles, most of which I have described. But you knew this, and you know there is more—too much more.

"There is a time. A moment in time, an occasion that not everyone has. But it occurs as a defining moment. Who can explain the feeling, the knowledge that it is what it is while it happens? Is it Divine Providence? Who knows? This defining moment of ecstasy and terror, or one or the other. Does a person ever realize the moment until after? Or, is it as Fernando Pessoa, the author of *The Book of Disquiet*, wrote a year before his death:

> *In this world where we forget*
> *We are shadows of who we are.*

"Death or, rather, the moment of death—all humans think about it. Sylvester was a man who had fought and survived, and who fought because he had to be there—not for any love of war. But to come to the point of death, resigned to let it happen, yet survive the moment enough to recall the feeling? Sylvester had that experience and his spirit survived in his family."

"As I am now."

"Yes, in a way. You have come to a different experience, but it is very similar."

"How? How is this different?"

"Perhaps you are in a coma, or maybe a dream. The experience is the same, but the result may be different."

"You mean I am not—"

"We shall see. I cannot help but think that all this dialogue has a reason. Every person's journey is different. Your individualism will not disappear with your death."

"No?"

"No."

"So now I am neither dead nor alive? To be determined, but no matter because my individualism will survive in either case?"

"I appreciate your sarcasm. You miss the point. You are more than your physical self. The burials of King Raedwald and Sylvester are real. Yet, their memories live on: a king, found by an archaeologist, and a young soldier, thought to be forgotten—save for the lips of a nephew he never met. Your grandfather.

"In life you worry about reputation and what people think of you. Are you good or bad? Decent or not? And so on. None of those traits have anything to do with your physical self. And, in fact, for every person, those traits, whatever they may be, survive their physical death. People live beyond their death. Life continues in the spirit of the person and the influence he or she had. In short, the memory of you can live for infinity. No, it is not the caterpillar-to-butterfly analogy, but something more profound."

"And simple."

"Yes."

# Existence
## (Ralph Foster)

A MAN AND A BOY WERE ON A CAMPING OUTING in the old man's pickup truck with a makeshift camper. The boy loved his grandfather, and Ralph returned the affection for his daughter's son. But for some reason on a highway north through Santa Fe and Española in New Mexico, the old man pulled off to a rest stop and announced, "We will spend the night here."

This was strange because this had not happened in the previous outings. The boy wondered why here when many nice campsites could be found within a half hour from where they were. But he said nothing.

They got an early start the next day and continued north toward Taos. Within minutes, they dropped off a plateau into the Velarde Valley with its lush orchards of various fruits. Then they entered a canyon with steep walls, cut by the Rio Grande, a river with headwaters in the Mountains of Colorado that flows into the Gulf of

Mexico. They paralleled the river on their left side as they drove north.

Every so often, the old man stopped and studied … what? He looked at the river or perhaps the other side. Finally, after three or four stops, the old man pointed out to his grandson what looked like an old roadbed on the other side of the river.

"Do you see that, son?"

"What, Grandpa?"

"That roadbed."

"Was that where the old railroad ran?"

"No. It was to be a road. This road. The one we are on now."

"Was it ever finished?"

"It doesn't look like it. But I want you to know that I worked on that road right over there." He pointed across the river.

The boy let the man continue.

"I was tied to another man with a chain and forced to work there. Then I—we—escaped."

That was the beginning of a story that Ralph told his grandson only once. But it was a story that needed telling the multiple times that the grandson continued to share throughout his life.

Ralph lived a fairly normal life. Vibrant, healthy, and tall, he worked a farm to support his family. Aside from his wife Viola's local reputation as a faith healer, he lived a normal, if not carefree, life in Burkburnett, Texas where he lived in the late 1930s. The town did not promise a bright future. Its oil boom days had passed, and in the last ten years the population had shrunk from a high of around twenty thousand people to an ever-decreasing number of 3,281 when a count was taken in 1936.

The town is situated ten miles north of Wichita Falls next to the Red River that also was the southern border of Oklahoma and on the east edge of the Great Plains. The combination of World War I and the crash of the national economy—along with the stock market—spelled "doom" for the town's heyday. Those events seemed distant and, moreover, incomprehensible to a person who languished in the town where most of the one-story businesses that lined the main street had closed. Still, as long as he could find an odd job or two, Ralph felt secure and content.

Then the weather, or lack of it, changed everything. A drought struck and fertile fields turned into dust. The persistent winds finished the job. No longer able to sustain his family, Ralph needed to find a job and Burkburnett had none to offer. California beckoned.

Like many of his neighbors, Ralph planned with his wife. He would go to California, "the Golden State," get employed, and send for the family as soon as he could. Of course, getting there was another problem. He had never had enough money to buy a car, so he decided on the next obvious solution. He would hop onto one of the freight trains heading north to connect with the east and, importantly, the western lines. After a little research and a couple of days watching others hop a train, he jumped onboard himself.

Everything went well initially. He made it north and was able to hop a train heading west. All seemed good. He would be in California in a couple of days. But the train pulled to a stop in a railyard in Tucumcari, New Mexico. He had no reason for concern at first, but the voices of men and barking of dogs caught him by surprise. The car door slid open to expose three uniformed men in the sunlight.

Taken from the train and held until the men finished their search, Ralph and six other men were confronted by a filthy-looking man in a dirty, sweat-and-tobacco-stained brown uniform. His eyes were so close-set they appeared crossed. He projected an attitude with no regard for person or law except when it existed for his personal need. His taciturn expression, sloppy demeaner, and a stomach that extended from his chin to an overwhelmed belt buckle, left a clear impression of the man's dishonesty. Except for his obesity, he could have been a pirate in another time and place. With a sense of pleasure, if not satisfaction, he notified the men of their arrest and that they would be taken to a Justice of Peace for a hearing.

If there were any doubt about their plight, the Justice of the Peace made it clear. Holding court in a renovated trailer set up alongside the tracks in a dirt parking lot, the small, clumsily built, old man whose understated jaw accented a perturbing lower lip hiding a wad of tobacco smiled cynically, pretending that he was preoccupied. His exposed brown and yellow teeth put an exclamation point on the matter. Then, in a voice artificially lowered to project a semblance of authority, he spoke to no one in particular: "What do we have here?"

The sheriff answered, "More vagrants."

The judge's whimsical smile expanded. Ralph thought he might laugh.

"You boys looking for work, huh?"

No one answered. The smile turned into a frown, and the sheriff sniffed.

"These boys were on their way to California."

"Well, then," the judge said, looking at the sheriff. "We will save you boys some time and trouble. No need to go that far. We've worked 'nough here. Buster—"

*Naturally,* Ralph thought. *A perfect name for the man.*

"How many in the bus? Twenty? Is that right?"

The sheriff tucked his thumbs in his belt. "That 'bout right. This makes, uh—"

"Twenty-seven."

"Yes."

"Enough to send them. This will be a good payday."

Then, the judge turned and spit his tobacco onto the floor.

"Well, boys, I find you guilty of vagrancy, and I sentence you to hard labor. Buster, have the boys bring the chains."

Then, he repeated his sinister smile and said, "Enjoy your stay in New Mexico."

One of the men spoke up: "We are American! You can't do this!"

The minuscule judge did not like that objection.

"Buster, show him your club."

Buster pulled out his baton.

"You see, boys. You in my court and I can do what I want. Next one who speaks out—well, Buster here is goin' ta rap that club of his 'round your head. D'ya hear me?"

With that, Buster stood over them as his deputies attached leg-irons around each man's ankle, pairing them off in twos. As such, they were paraded to an old bus. Ralph's dream of going to California and calling for his family was the last thing on his mind.

The matter of thirst, hunger, and suppressing heat became a more immediate concern. They were being treated like animals. Finally, the man chained to and sitting next to him spoke.

"Hi. May name is Dennis Pasterboy. I gagiated from the eight grade."

Ralph looked at his partner, a younger, small man with matted black hair and bulging brown eyes. He introduced himself, choosing not to reveal that he had a high school education.

After almost five hours with one stop where the men were allowed to relieve themselves, the bus pulled up to a stop in a dry canyon next to a river. They were ordered out and escorted onto a foot bridge to cross the river. A new set of armed men, not in uniforms, met them and signed some papers presented to them by the sheriff's deputies. Buster was too important to take the trip.

The new guards looked disengaged, maybe tired. At the very least, Ralph discerned that they were not happy.

"Okay, guys, see those tents up there?" The guard pointed up river. "Welcome home. Let's go. Move!"

So they walked, still chained to one another, to a tent filled with cots, some obviously occupied but their inhabitants missing.

Assigned to their cots, they were instructed about the schedule and warned not to think about escaping: "If the Rio don' drown ya, we'll catch ya. Then you'll be ours fo' sure."

The head guard then ordered the chains taken off and had the men clean themselves as best they could in the river. Ralph learned that they would be digging a road next to the Rio Grande. By paying attention and listening to the company's employees, the real ones, he was able to figure out that he was somewhere between Santa Fe and Taos in northern New Mexico.

Each day they were given pickaxes and shovels, chained to each other in twos again, and set to work. They picked and shoveled through dirt and lava rock. Some had tasks of loading the wheelbarrows; others moved the full loads to a designated spot. Water, if given a chance to drink, came from the river, and that moment doubled for an opportunity to cool off.

It did not take long for Ralph to figure out that the unhappy guards were not too observant. He studied their routines and realized that there would be plenty of opportunities for an escape. But he had to share his plans with Dennis, who was almost always chained to him.

"Can you swim?" he asked Dennis one day.

"Nope. Never saw the purpose."

"Want to escape?"

"Ya heard what the man said. I don' know."

"Do you want to stay here forever?"

"Well, no. That true."

"Well, then, can you trust me? We will leave tonight."

Ralph had to explain why they would be leaving so soon: "The longer we wait, the more chance to be found out."

And with that, he received a simple "Oh" for an answer.

Thus, after the guards had taken their full share of drink, played a round of cards, and almost got into a fight, the moment came that Ralph had been waiting for. Instead of paying attention to their jobs, the guards dosed off. Moreover, they slept far away enough that the noise of a slight footstep would not disturb them.

Ralph and Dennis left downriver to the bridge and, after crossing the river, headed further south to the first community they encountered. Later in life, Ralph would learn that they had made it to Velarde. Still attached to each other, they came to an orchard before day break. They rested among the trees, eating apples and always alert for any hint of pursuit. None could be discerned.

A shed at the back of a house gave them hope that they might find something inside to help them get rid of their chain. But the sun had risen and, as is normal for any person working crops or animals, movement in the house indicated that they should hurry. Dennis could not be moved fast enough, and when he did move, it usually was clumsily. As Ralph learned, Dennis did not know left from right, so a wrong turn walked him into some tools— the noise of which could not be avoided, and they were confronted by a shirtless man with a shotgun pointed directly at them.

"Come out of there. *¿Quién estan?*"

"Don't shoot. We're unarmed."

That was all Ralph knew to say. Dennis was too terrified to speak. Once out in the open, Ralph continued talking as the short, darkhaired man noticed their chains.

Then, he added: "We escaped from the road gang."

"I know what you did. You are not the first. Why are you in my shed? To hide?"

"No."

"Then what?"

"We were looking for a tool to get these chains off of us."

Ralph paused. Suddenly it dawned upon him. This was an unusual conversation.

"Will you take us back? They should be looking for us by now."

The man lowered his rifle and revealed a mouth full of straight white teeth as he smiled.

"Take you back? Only if you want me to. As I said, you are not the first. The road company will not expend time or money looking for you."

"Are you sure?"

"They will replenish you with the next bus load. Simple, huh?"

With the gun lowered and no longer a threat, the three men looked at each other, not knowing what to say next.

Finally, the man spoke, "I am Esteban Manzanares."

A much-relieved Ralph introduced himself and Dennis, after which Esteban said, "You can call me Steve."

Steve helped them out of their chains and gave them a simplified geography lesson drawing a map in the dirt. Then, he took them in his house and treated them to some coffee, eggs, meat of some kind, and red chili. Ralph had an easier time with the latter than did Dennis—who, after one bite, refused to try more. He merely shook his head, scrunched his face, and said "No."

He told them that they could get back to Texas a number of ways. They could go south to Santa Fe and then hitch a ride on U.S. 66 back to Amarillo. Or, they could cross the mountains from Taos and get to Raton where they could hitch a ride or take the bus into Texas.

Dennis opted for going south. Esteban agreed to take him as far as the next town.

Ralph felt it safer to take the Taos route. Besides, Esteban had piqued his attention describing the route through the mountains: "At Taos, take the road to Cimarron. There is no bus. You will have to find a ride. It is too far to walk and it can get cold at night. From Cimarron, you will know how to get to Raton."

Ralph could not thank Esteban enough. Esteban merely shrugged his shoulders and said, "*Como le dije.* As I said, you are not the first." The three of them hopped into Esteban's old pickup and drove a half mile to a store on the village's main road. Esteban went inside and returned with a man who introduced himself as, "Your *tocayo*! My name is Rafael. Stay with me tonight, and tomorrow we will go to Taos."

Esteban and Dennis drove off to the south, and Ralph spent the night before an eye-opening trip of an hour and half to Taos. They left Velarde with its orchards, climbed up the canyon, then turned into a place that Rafael called Embudo.

He stopped at a bar both to check his vehicle and to have a drink. When he noticed Ralph standing there with empty hands out, he struck a deal. "If you check the radiator and clean the windows, I will pay you with a drink, *¿'ta bien?*"

Ralph did not need Spanish lessons to understand. The drink was especially good. Taos sat at the foot of the mountain and looked like a small town of mud houses— *adobe*, they called it. He never got to explore the town, though, as Rafael let him out south of it on a highway that darted off east toward the mountains.

"Amigo, stick your thumb out. It is the way here. You will not wait long. *Buena suerte!* Good luck! This is the road to Cimarron. *Vaya con Dios*. Go with God."

Within a half hour Ralph was sitting on the back of an old truck heading through the mountain on his way to Raton. The mountains overwhelmed him. Ralph could not get over the forests—pine trees so thick that in the distance they looked like a lawn. He had never seen anything like that. He came from a treeless, now-barren land. The lush vegetation! The fresh, dry air! It seemed as the dreary world he left behind did not exist here. Even the jarring ride could not distract him from his appreciation for the landscape he passed through.

Raton, a coal mining town with a railroad stop and a national highway running down its main street, appealed to Ralph. The town had a mountain feel. It sat at the southern end of a pass that rose almost eight thousand feet. The highway over it could be closed for snow and ice in the winter, but when open, the number of cars traveling to and from Colorado meant income for the small town.

No business profited more than the local gas station where Ralph found work. The station did a hefty business selling gas, but what really brought in money were the skilled mechanics working there who could fix the many brakes burned out from the steep roads nearby. Ralph was hired to repair brakes. His experience with machines and tools was obvious to the station owner, and for almost two years he worked there, earning enough money to save a little. At first he hesitated to contact his Viola for fear that he would be detected. But over time, he was able to reach her via telephone, not that she had one, but through various contacts. Then he wrote short letters. Eventually, he even went back to Burkburnett for a couple of extended visits.

Finally, he realized that he needed to leave Raton and return home permanently. But it did not take him long to realize that his initial sentiment about Burkburnett was correct. The place was dying, and he did not want to die with it. His wife agreed with him. Right when the war broke out, or maybe because it did, they moved to Amarillo where the government had opened some bomb factories.

But he could never forget the forests of northern New Mexico and probably talked too much about it. Despite the bad experience of the chain gang, his desire to get back there became obvious. However, his factory wage was not near enough to cover such a move.

After a couple of years, fate turned in their favor. Viola had healed a very wealthy oil man who was so convinced of her talent that he gave her and Ralph a large three-story house in downtown Amarillo. The place was so big that Ralph used part of the house as a flower shop, and in another part of the house, Viola sheltered unwed mothers. They used the shop to train the mothers in the business as a way to give them some skills.

However, the dream of the lush mountains persisted for Ralph, and, finally, he and Viola agreed to sell the house and use the money to move to the southern Rockies. Only, Ralph wanted more than he remembered. They scouted north of Taos into the San Luis Valley of southern Colorado where, outside of Alamosa, they used their savings to purchase a farm.

He and Viola suffered through winter in these high altitudes. Farming is not nearly as convenient in such a climate as it is in lower and warmer climates. And they were not particularly used to such weather. It did not take much time for them to realize that the dream of mountain living needed to be adjusted—and that prompted a move south, forsaking self-sufficiency on a farm.

Sometime after 1950, they moved to Albuquerque, New Mexico, where they purchased a house in the city's far east side nestled next to the mountains. Finally, place and opportunity combined to end the wanderlust life Ralph had come to lead. He was close enough to his beloved mountains and their forests. He could go camping or fishing any weekend. And if he wanted, he could revisit the never-completed road he had been forced to help construct. Or, he could go back to Alamosa and reminisce. Burkburnett and Amarillo were another matter, though. There is also no record of him returning to Tucumcari.

On a rare occasion, he brought up his experiences as a convicted vagrant to Viola. Hardly anyone else knew about that part of his life; Ralph had become a private man. Yet years later, when he noticed that one of his grandsons shared his love of the outdoors, Ralph could not resist encouraging the boy. He began to take him on excursions into the mountains of northern New Mexico and southern Colorado. Were it not for showing his grandson where he had once been unjustly condemned to work, his memory, his history, could have been lost to posterity. Instead, his grandson maintained the story and, moreover, was astute enough to understand that it revealed an interesting if overlooked part of Southwestern history.

# *Fate V*

THE STORY ENDED. Silence ensued. Then the spirit spoke.

"There is little difference between spirit and memory. If you have done nothing in life, you have left little memory and nothing of a spirit."

"Do nothing? Don't we all do something?"

"Our spirits work in mysterious ways. We wander and engage. We encounter other spirits, souls you could not imagine or meet in life. I suppose you would call it a mental process—that 'cosmic soul' we talked about. And, yes, it is particular to each individual. Some people live lives never encountering their true self, their unconscious being. And they never fulfill a destiny they will never know."

"We do good things and bad."

"Obviously. Serial killers. Adolf Hitler."

"And their spirits survive?"

"Yes. As memories, so we may learn from them, so their actions may never be repeated. I should explain. There are positive—"

"And negative."

"Yes. The two do not mix. Exactly. Unless the negative evolves to something positive, they are regulated to the unknown."

"This sounds like a vague concept of heaven and hell."

"I suppose. To spend eternity as a bad memory—well, yes. Listen, my friend, it is healthy to be friends with one's self. You are not the only one to become aware of your spirit. This is not some great, celestial secret."

"I should thank you?"

"But, you know, these spiritual encounters are not one on one. Yes, we encounter spirits of other individuals, but we also feed on concepts or, to put bluntly, the residue of another person's spiritual production. For example, I know we visited an old friend that you in life could never meet."

"Me? I'm dead or might be. How?"

"Oh, yes. Excuse me. I was attracted to the spirit of a creative mind. Rational as well. In this case, his spirit manifested in one of his literary creations. A protagonist."

"No, wait! His imaginary figures come alive?"

"Spiritually. Like your Quixote—or need I remind you of artists who speak through their paintings? You know that the story behind the art is just as fascinating as the work itself. Its origin is a part of its content. The

Spanish master Velasquez draws you into his art. Look at his *Las Meninas*. He paints himself looking at you, but he is actually looking at the royal couple reflected in the mirror behind him. That very concept inspired Salvador Dali. Sometimes these creative minds, spirits, almost reveal themselves. Cervantes, for example—remember Quixote's death scene? Shakespeare—well, imagine Macbeth talking to the skull or the message of Romeo and Juliet still not heeded. The magic realism so associated with Latin American literature. The magic—or spirit—is real. Remember the three ghosts Charles Dickens used in *A Christmas Carol*? I could go on."

"So could I. Handel claimed that his masterpiece *Messiah* came to him in a revelation!"

"And in science too. The physicist Neils Bohr, who won the Nobel Prize for physics in 1922 for his revelation of the structure of an atom—his discovery came to him in a dream when he saw an atom with electrons spinning around it, like the solar system. Even Einstein talked about dreams. You see?"

"How could I not? But—"

"No. Enough for now. Allow me to continue with my stories."

"I suppose I haven't a choice."

# *Curiosity*
# *(Arthur Conan Doyle)*

You may remember that back in the 1980s, at the height of the Cold War, a Korean Airliner 747 was shot down. North Korean missiles shot down that huge passenger jet. A few days after that tragedy, a friend happened to be in London, where he visited an old acquaintance at 221B Baker Street. As fortune would have it, he entered during a conversation between my acquaintance and his colleague, Dr. Watson. Apparently continued from a chance meeting at the Criterion Bar from whence both had just arrived, he thought it best to allow the conversation to run its course.

Watson sat looking upon my friend as his mentor, and listened.

"I have found that it is usually in the obvious matters that there is a field for the observation, and for the quick analysis of cause and effect, which gives charm to an investigation. Here we have a crime of international import in which the United States has established a very serious case against the Soviet Union."

"I cannot disagree," chimed Watson.

"The press, it seems, from what I gather, has compiled one of those simple cases—"

"Quite so."

"—and which I find are so extremely difficult."

"I could hardly imagine a more damning case," Watson remarked. "If ever circumstantial evidence pointed to a criminal, it does so here. The Soviets have admitted their crimes."

"The act, Watson, but no crime."

"What?"

"On behalf of his government, Gromyko admitted to the act but has not acquiesced to calling it a crime."

"I daresay Holmes, sometimes your reasoning and the methods by which you draw conclusions perplex me. Please do myself the honor and my curiosity the satisfaction of explaining this case."

Holmes fell into silence, his head sunk upon his breast, with the air of a man who is lost in thought. The puffs on his pipe were the only sounds to be heard. Finally, he lifted his head.

"I admire your gift for silence, Watson, for my own thoughts are not over-pleasant. Let us recap the story as the accuser would have us hear it. A passenger airliner, the so-called KAL-7, in flight from Alaska to South Korea, strayed off course into Soviet air space, where it was intercepted and shot down in a wanton act of murder.

The accuser claims that there is, for the moment, no explanation as to how KAL-7 went off course—that once the plane had strayed, no one was able to correct the error, and that the Soviets should have realized that a 747 jumbo jet could be nothing but a commercial airliner."

"And two hundred sixty-nine people were killed," added Watson.

"Yes, and from all accounts no radio communication, with one minor exception, occurred between KAL-7's crew and anyone, from the moment the airliner entered Soviet space until the tragic culmination. Have I gone astray, Watson?"

"No, Holmes. You are quite on course, although I have no idea where you will lead us."

"Before we look closer at this case, let us agree on one other fact. The act of shooting down the plane after it had entered Soviet air space did not violate international law."

"Did not violate law," Watson whispered over a cup of tea, "but certainly mocked even the meanest of moral standards."

"That all depends, but more on that anon. First, let us establish the context in which this incident took place. The litigants are leading rivals on the international scene. The new Soviet leadership has worked hard to project a new image of moderation in a bid to stymie NATO deployment of United States missiles in western Europe. Leadership in the United States embarked on a hardline policy toward communist aggression but was anxious to continue negotiations with the Soviets. The KAL-7 incident disrupted a promising round of arms talks initiated by the Soviet offer to 'liquidate' part of its missile force."

"But this does not point to the events."

"There is more that will perhaps shed increased light on the matter. Soviet defenses guarding La Perouse Strait, over which this event occurred, are important. Russia's main fleet base at Vladivostok is integral to the whole Pacific theater of operations. The area around La Perouse had undergone a recent expansion program. Among other ships, at least twenty-five nuclear missile submarines normally pass through the strait. In a war, the strait would be the direct route for the deployment of the Soviet Pacific fleet. The strait is of singular importance to the Soviet Bear and, thus, of consequence to United States strategic planning. La Perouse narrow is what the United States Navy un-euphemistically calls a 'choke point.'"

"Important indeed," added Watson. "Significant enough for the United States to monitor aircraft movements and military communications almost thirty years past."

"More than that, my good doctor. The United States deliberately commenced probe flights to elicit a Soviet response and to ascertain the extent of Soviet defenses in the region. The KAL-7 incident occurred within the context of an aggressive American effort to gather information—'develop technical intelligence penetration'

I believe they call it—in the Sea of Okhotsk. Prior to the case at hand, there had been more than a score of such incidents, many of them recorded in considerable detail."

Watson interrupted, "Does that include that other Korean airliner?"

"From the Soviet point of view, precisely."

"The Russians forced that airliner down after hitting it with a missile."

Holmes gave a whimsical smile. "Again Doctor, you have hit the nail on the head."

Watson kept to himself that he did not care for Holmes's patronizing tone but accepted the habit as harmless.

Holmes continued, "And that happened only five years ago. Such precedent on top of years of monitoring should have forewarned pilots of the Soviet Union's sensitivity of violators of that country's air space."

Holmes paused to toke on his pipe. "And what can you surmise of the KAL-7 pilot?"

The words came out of a swirl of pipe smoke. Not waiting for a reply, he answered his own question: "That he should have known better. As a retired South Korean Air Force pilot and a five-year veteran of the route on which he went astray, he was privy to all that preceded. I might add that the co-pilot had the same experience and should have had similar knowledge of that area's intricacies.

"Allow me to surmise further. I do not believe that KAL-7 was lost. As stated, the pilots were too experienced to wander more than five hundred miles off course. And experts have already ruled out equipment malfunction. An earlier report of problems with the radio and one of the aircraft's compass devices was alleviated by mechanics in Alaska, where all was declared to be in order. Three on-board computers separately fed the aircraft's navigational system. Now ponder this, Watson! That plane's computers are designed to withstand outside interference and to alert pilots to any deviation from course—amazing."

A voice interrupted: "Wait a minute! Am I supposed to believe that a nineteenth century fictional character is solving a case about a late twentieth century jet? Flight was but a dream in his day or his creator's."

The spirit answered, "Ah, you have much to learn. Time is of secondary importance in our world. It does not matter. Consciousness is timeless. The limits of chronological order do not exist. Life is a sequence of dreams revealing inner life."

"But—wait! What happened to my conscience? Why are you…?"

"Listen and learn. Accept what you are witnessing as a matter of faith. May we continue?"

"Faithfully."

A moment of silence ensued. Perhaps for emphasis. Then, the spirit continued.

"Can you imagine such a system for a hansom on London's streets?" Holmes said. "The only problem at this point is, as the United States's president asked, was the information correct when it went into the computers? This, of course, has been answered and verified. The information was correct. After that, experts claim, the 'redundant inertial navigational systems'—a rather impressive name, I should think—are virtually 'failsafe.'"

Watson had finished his tea. "Then how…"

"The only conclusion, good doctor, is that for once, and for reasons unknown to us, the aircraft was intentionally off course. And given the information already before us, it is not an unsafe inference to conclude that this flight was another probe into the Soviet air defenses."

"But that is incredible! You conclude that a pilot—pilots—will jeopardize over two hundred lives?"

Holmes sighed. "My dear sir, the people who are in the international intelligence business not only will jeopardize lives but have killed continuously for their information. In this case, there was a chance no one would be harmed. As we know, the conclusion proved quite different. Surprised? Pshaw! The same people have hired assassins, supplied armies, mined fields and harbors. One needs only to recall the assassination of a certain South Vietnamese leader or to consider the recent affairs in Chile. In fact, the Bay of Pigs episode…. Yes, anyone, including our pilots, could easily be misled by the hard combination of money, patriotism—remember, they both had previous military careers—and assurances of the task's safety."

"All of which is of no use to them now."

"Obviously so."

"Your scenario explains much."

"Explain on, Watson."

"The Soviet reaction comes foremost to mind. Then, the constant alternating of radio transmissions! Why, an American spy plane was up at the same time! The uneven radio contacts from KAL-7, and, at times, radio silence. Furthermore…."

Watson's protracted list innervated his companion, who now stood in front of a very cluttered table. While jerking his brier out of his mouth, he cut Watson short: "Even more damning is the aircraft's route after it had strayed off course. When it was first sighted beyond international airspace, the ship was headed toward highly sensitive Soviet military and naval installations at Petropavlovsk.

"When the Soviet interceptors caught up with the ship, it appeared to be correcting its erroneous route but then suddenly swung back over Soviet territory—this time, toward Sakhalin Island, where the Soviets had even more sensitive military encampments. When a second wave of fighters sighted the aircraft, it had gained altitude, as verified by a KAL-7 radio transmission to Tokyo, and was leaving Soviet airspace for the second time. Its lights were on."

Holmes paused as he unconsciously placed his unlit pipe in his mouth, then said, "Let me correct that. The aircraft's strobe lights were on. Were they on before? Who knows? And why did the Soviets report them off?"

Another pause.

"Perhaps the Soviets were mystified that no cabin lights were on."

"Really, Holmes! How do you know that?"

"Experienced conjecture, Watson. The Soviet pilot reports the strobes were on and was silent about any other lights. Cabin lights would have been noted. The lack thereof must have raised Soviet suspicions. It seems inconceivable that not one of almost three hundred passengers did not have an overhead light illuminated."

Holmes paused again, lost in thought. Then, he added, "Now two points worth noting here. First, the airliner changed course and later changed altitude. The suddenness and non-uniform manner in which these changes occurred indicate that the craft was flown manually. Secondly, the radio transmission to Tokyo."

Watson leaned forward, utterly transfixed on the slender speaker.

"One of the KAL-7 pilots radioed for the purpose of informing Tokyo air controllers that he was changing altitude. Again, evidence that the pilot was in control and that the radio worked."

Holmes strolled across the room to the fireplace and continued his lecture: "Let us examine one last piece to this puzzle as it is now before us. The question of radio problems is primary. Problems? Hardly. This is shown false by the example just enumerated. Furthermore, the radio was checked in Alaska."

Watson jumped up. "Newspaper reports have more accounts of radio transmissions."

"I believe you are on the right scent, Watson. Indeed, after leaving Alaska, the ground controllers received word on three different occasions from KAL-7. At two checkpoints the airliner relayed information to another airliner that it was on course. Why did they not radio direct? The papers postulate that KAL-7 was already off course and out of range."

"So, it sent back wrong information?"

"Yes, but the plot thickens. Between the two relayed transmissions, KAL-7 radioed directly to ground control by using a high frequency radio that had a greater range than the UHF normally used. Again, pilots and radios are functioning. Curiously, an airliner traveling in the opposite direction received no answer to its radio inquiries."

"To say the least, inconsistent," agreed Watson.

"A deliberate attempt, I am afraid, to mislead ground control and the world that KAL-7 is lost and having radio problems. Unfortunately, the deception is proof to an opposite conclusion."

"This is a terrible—"

"Do not be hasty, Watson. Not all the facts have surfaced. Experience demonstrates what the odd twist to a case can do to its conclusion. Even with the assumption that my conjecturing is correct, we cannot judge too harshly—again, for lack of information. We have no knowledge that the intelligence gathered was not worth the loss of life. Being a humanitarian personally, I would not wage that it was so. Furthermore, any rational person must assume that American intelligence felt, at worst, that the aircraft would be forced down and eventually allowed to leave. On that assumption, the turn of events and our deductions have pointed to a serious miscalculation. Finally, and most obvious, this is not a closed case."

Watson poured some more tea. "I suppose in matters such as these, the case is never closed."

Again, Holmes's chin fell onto his chest. After some seconds of thought, he stirred, tucked his hands into his smoking jacket, and replied: "The colonies have always held up the virtues of their system of jurisprudence for the world to view. 'Innocent until proven guilty.' Yet, within the international arena, as illustrated by this tragic but peculiar case, the defendant has been guilty until proven innocent. There is a double damnation here because the evidence cannot prove guilt. Indeed, the circumstantial facts, such as they are, point more to the accuser. Would that I could live long enough to hear the complete truth."

"If it ever be known, I would not be surprised to hear that both sides bear the blame."

"Quite so, my dear Watson. But let us not overlook the base message of this case. We cannot help but note the high stakes and sinister possibilities of international intrigue."

The conversation ended and the imagery of the story faded.

"That last comment is curious. How could he wish to live long enough when he is here now?"

"The subconscious sometimes thinks in the present, unaware that the body is dead. It may not realize the context of its existence. In this case, the thoughts are yours and the words come from your readings of Doyle's books. Your mind, your subconscious put them together. So, you projected that he would live long enough. In its way, he is expressed through you.

"And you have more to share because while sharing coffee at a local culinary shop in Santa Fe, a letter came to you."

"It did? I don't remember that."

"In your imagination."

"Oh."

"The letter came from London and it completes the story:

> *My good friend:*
>
> *Since our last visit, we have been on many an adventure. Nonetheless, during a recent infrequent lull, Holmes asked me to inquire of you about the possibility of publishing the KAL-7 account. He felt sufficient enough time had passed and thought the recent refusal of the United States to recognize any World Court judgment relative to the mining of Nicaragua's harbor would make an excellent paradoxical context. Please be assured, dear friend, that Holmes joins me in anxiously awaiting the fruit of your efforts with abated breath.*
>
> *We remain and are anxious to be,*
> *Your most obedient servants at your liege,*
>
> *Watson and Holmes*

## Fate VI

"Nice story, but what?"

"Exactly, a story on your mind for years. Somehow, it will prevail as a memory, a message, or part of the formation of your attitude toward governments. In many ways. You may even write the story for the benefit of others."

"This is surreal. Is this death or am I dreaming? Am I going mad?"

"Except for the physical aspect, there is no difference."

"Hearing voices, talking to myself?"

"Everyone hears voices. Some listen and learn. Where do our ideas come from? And, yes, this is surreal— or, more precisely, surrealism, magical realism."

"Surrealism?"

"Defined as the physic automatism in its pure state in which a person tries to express himself verbally, or the written word, or any other manner the actual functioning of thought. It is based on the belief in an undefined reality of certain forms of previously neglected associations revealed in a dream or in the disinterested play of thought."

"So, which are you? A dream? The dis... what?"

"The disinterested play of thought. You are beginning to understand."

"Really? Here we are in some weirdness, and I understand?"

"You have posed the big question. After this epiphany, as you would call it, what will you do with it?"

"I am a historian. This hardly calls for a footnote."

"Then write without footnotes. You do write, yes?"

"Yes."

"So, express yourself."

"But if I am dead..."

"There is more to share. There is no need to rush the inevitable."

# Irony Again
## *(Monica Sosaya and Marilyn Sprowl)*

MONICA WAS A LONELY WOMAN. Naturally attractive with dark hair, blue eyes bordering on hazel, a nose more prominent than it needed to be, and a slight figure. Boys found her attractive, and her parents, especially her strict mother, knew it. This fact, in the context of her equally attractive older sister, who was her mother's favorite, amounted to an unhappy life. Her parents at once lorded it over her and ridiculed her. She was their "ugly duckling." But worse, they overlooked her independent, if stubborn, nature. And that, in her late teens, she was unhappy.

Then, into her life came a rather remarkable person. Like her, this woman had an independent streak. Marilyn was a younger daughter with an elder sister and strict parents. At first, Marilyn seemed a little strange. After all, Monica was a descendant of a multi-generation Hispanic New Mexican family. Marilyn was an Anglo, not one of her kind. But Marilyn had married a cousin and she, maybe seven years older, had come to New Mexico for reasons Monica appreciated and admired.

Marilyn came from a middle-class family in northern Ohio, lived a normal childhood, didn't get into trouble, played the clarinet in her high school band, and hung out with her girlfriends. Still, she had a sense of adventure and an unfounded confidence to go along with it. Her older sister's departure for California was an added incentive as well as example.

The outbreak of war at the end of 1941 gave her the opportunity to leave. Within months, the navy created the Women Accepted for Volunteer Emergency Service, known as the WAVES. It was a naval reserve to enlist women to serve in non-combatant roles, thus freeing up men for other duty. Marilyn sized the opportunity, enlisted in the WAVES and left home.

She was discharged at the war's end. With nowhere else to go or do, she returned home, but it was too late. As military service, if not just time away from home, will do, she needed to be on her own. So, she and one of her navy girlfriends decided to go to an exotic place and chose New Mexico. They would use the GI Bill to pay their expenses while they attended the University of New Mexico. As could be done at the time, they donned their uniforms and hitched a free ride to Albuquerque, thanks to the U.S. Army Air Corps.

They found the place different enough, but after waiting too long in line to enroll in the university, they became displeased. They asked, "Is there a smaller school in a smaller town someone could recommend?"

Las Vegas was the answer—Las Vegas, New Mexico and New Mexico Highlands University, "a teachers' college," only two or three hours north. They could get there by train or hitch a ride. Fortuitously, some young Army Air Corps pilots overheard the conversation. Perhaps with ulterior motives, the young men offered to fly Marilyn and her friend to Las Vegas. This could be done as long as the two women wore their uniforms. The two women agreed.

Thus, a few days later, Marilyn and her friend flew to Las Vegas in a B-17 flying fortress bomber that the pilots landed on Las Vegas's dirt landing strip. The place was not an airport, just a strip and a couple of hangers that looked like barns. If they had wanted something different, this fit the bill. Mountains hovered close by to the north and west. They did not appear as majestic as the large mountain overlooking Albuquerque. Then, in every other direction flat land extended as far as they could see. And the town, their destination, remained a mystery.

The young pilots questioned, "Well, ladies, are you sure? We can take you back."

Marilyn was not sure at first what she wanted to do, but her determination won. "No, I mean yes, this is it. We will stay here. At least—"

"We will escort you into town to make sure you are okay," one officer said.

"Thank you, and thank you for the lift, but we can do."

Another officer laughed. "Of that, I am sure. We will go with you 'cause I don't want to spend the rest of my life wondering what happened to you."

The first officer, the one Marilyn supposed was the co-pilot, joined in. "Don't worry, the plane has to be returned today. It's not our property, ya know."

One of what looked like three staff at the landing strip drove them the couple of miles into the town and to the university. While not impressive, the two-story stone administration building was a welcome sight. And their expectations were met.

A friendly greeting prefaced a welcomed reception. They parted with army pilots who wished them well. A ride back to the airstrip was arranged. Within the next couple of hours, they were registered into classes and were left in their dorm room.

Then began their real adventure. The small New Mexico Highlands University was full of veterans, recently returned from the war. The classes were full, but the students had other things on their minds. They had suffered a war. Most of them first-hand. They had survived and could not resist the urge to let off steam, celebrate. The town's bars and small clubs did a booming business. And the small town's population had increased by almost a third. Of necessity, much of the action took place off of campus, centered on the town's plaza, a square defined by nineteenth-century buildings. The heavily shaded— some would even say quaint—plaza hardly spoke of the years past when the famous Bat Masterton tended bar in one of its saloons. Or when the permanent gallows in the plaza facilitated the hanging of more men than in any other town in the west. Moreover, none of Las Vegas's latest population of students cared to know.

It was an exciting time. Football season had begun. The games were another excuse to gather with newly made friends and find a party. Marilyn and her friend stayed up late and slept in. They had the foresight to schedule their classes in the late morning and afternoon. Weekends, of course, were a different matter—and this was especially so when the traveling carnival came to town.

So, it happened after a late Saturday afternoon when Marilyn slept in and decided to spend the day washing cloths and cleaning her shared apartment. Just taking it easy. But her planned tranquility was interrupted when her roommate rushed through the door with two or three other people that she only knew by sight. Marilyn focused on a boy whose face was cut-up, one eye swollen, and with what looked like a bloody nose or cut lip—she could not tell.

Naturally concerned for the guy, she asked, "What happened?"

"A fight," was the quick answer.

"A fight? Where? Who?"

"No! No. Not what you think. At the carnival. He won the prize! Fifty dollars! Or, I think so. Tony, did you get the money?"

Tony looked up through his smashed face with a wry grin. That was his answer.

Marilyn brought out towels and water and helped clean Tony up. She learned that he had lasted three rounds boxing with the "carnival oaf." One of his friends, who introduced himself as Bill, explained that the "oaf" had something in his gloves and was "way bigger than Tony."

But, he added, Tony never went down and stood up to the man, "even cutting him up a little."

Tony finally spoke to no one in general. "Hey, this is nothing. He cheated, but we knew that going in. I lasted the three rounds, got in some shots, and won the prize money. I think we need to celebrate."

Marilyn stared at him in disbelief and said, "You are in no condition to celebrate."

Tony looked at his blood-stained T-shirt. "Oh this! Not now. After I shower and change. A cold beer is what I need."

With Marilyn, Tony got a cold beer and a short relationship that resulted in a marriage and five children. Tony, who had been a boxer in the Marine Corp before arriving in Las Vegas, was from an extended Hispanic family in Santa Fe. His brother, a priest, married Tony and Marilyn, and Marilyn was welcomed into the family—which included Tony's first cousin Monica.

Marilyn and Tony asked Monica to babysit their first-born, a task she performed with joy. Marilyn and Monica were roughly the same age and they developed a deep friendship. Monica found Marilyn's stories of leaving home and joining the navy fascinating.

Finally, one day Marilyn had heard enough about Monica's relationship with her mother. She looked directly into Monica's face and said, "Why don't you enlist in the WAVES?"

With Monica stunned into silence, Marilyn continued, "It is a job. Better than baby-sitting. You need to leave home, and with the WAVES, you will travel."

Despite her parents' shock, Monica enlisted with the Women Accepted for Volunteer Emergency Service. For the rest of her life, she did not hesitate to proclaim that Marilyn had saved her. Monica went on to be a prolific artist and, of course, a lifelong friend to Marilyn.

Marilyn and Tony moved to Ohio, then back to Santa Fe and, finally to Los Angeles where Tony went to law school. They had had another boy and three girls. Tony became a judge in the Angel City and is probably most noted as the man who signed the arrest warrants for and then arraigned Charles Manson and his family.

# *Fate VII*

"So you see, distance and time are related," the spirit said. "They create context, which, in turn, makes sense of cause and effect. The war changed peoples' lives. It had many effects, caused many things to happen. And traveling from desperate places brought people together."

"Fate."

"Yes, fate, but also action. Time and travel do not on their own create events. Individuals have to react, and that, finally, makes history—or, if you will, memories."

A deep, resonant, but clear voice interrupted—"*¡No me olvides!* Do not forget me!"

"Grand Jefe! How could I! Such memories. We never parted. And every time I do a barbeque, an *asado*, I think about you."

"*Sí, yo sé. Pero basta. Cuéntanos la historia.* Yes, I know. But enough. Tell the story."

# Survival
## (El Gran Jefe)

In San Juan, a city in western Argentina at the foot of the Andes Mountains, a young Vicente López was hanging out with friends avoiding the summer's heat in a courtyard during the evening of January 15, 1944. At 8:52 PM an earthquake struck, and his life changed forever.

At the time, San Juan had a population of ninety thousand inhabitants and was a town of mostly adobe structures that could not withstand the force of a seven- to eight-magnitude on the Richter scale. Ninety percent of the buildings were destroyed, ten thousand people died, and an approximate one third of the remaining population was left homeless. The catastrophe caused many families to scatter in confusion. Around one thousand children suddenly became orphans. People in despair roamed the street looking for missing family members or friends. Some painted names of their missing family members on walls.

Young Vicente, who was twelve years old, had been left in a children's home by his mother, whose husband had abandoned her. She was unable to provide for the child and thought it best to take this action. As was customary during the height of summer in that arid, hot place, the children were outside playing when they were interrupted by a sudden roar that quickly culminated with a loud boom when the earth jolted and shook. As a result of being outdoors, the children survived. Vicente and the others were brought together by obviously frightened and preoccupied caretakers. They would spend the night outdoors, without food and wondering what would happen next.

Vicente did not remember what happened next, except that he and another boy, whose name was Rafael, were the oldest, so they were designated by some adults to go out into the streets to learn more about what had happened. When they left the property, they saw the horrible results of the earthquake. Vicente remembers that he and Rafael were set to work scrambling through the rubble and into spaces looking for survivors, encountering some of the dead. They saw maimed and mangled people both alive and not. Then, Vicente was tasked with assisting nuns who were working in outdoor makeshift hospitals. He helped wrap bandages, set splints, replace gauze, do anything the sisters asked of him. He saw people maimed, in pain, some desperate, others determined. It was an experience that he would never forget.

Nor was he forgotten, because his mother survived and thought only about her son. She went to the children's home to find a partial building with nobody around. She was told that no bodies were found there and little else. *What had become of the children?* she wondered. She wanted her child back, but it was not to happen in the immediate aftermath of the town's destruction. With no help, she could only do what many others did: wonder about him, call out his name, search among homeless children, and check the posted casualty lists. In her desperation, she did not think to go to the authorities, who had put Vicente to work.

Eventually, Vicente and the other children were sent to the care of an orphanage in Mendoza, approximately eighty miles south of San Juan. With any luck he would be adopted and be able to live a somewhat normal life. However, a couple of opportunities did not work out. For one reason or another, the families or Vicente did not get along, so he was returned to the orphanage.

The third attempt, however, succeeded. An upper middle-class couple took him home for a "test period" over a weekend. They liked the boy, and he liked them. They understood what he had been through. They wanted to make a home for him, and they set a date to sign the adoption papers before a judge in court. Life for Vicente had improved, and he was happy. Thoughts about his mother, while always there, had faded. A new chapter in his life was about to begin.

Still, his mother persisted. Back in San Juan, every day she poured over government lists of newly identified survivors. Then, the government started publishing lists of orphaned children and, as the information became available, what had become of them. After months that seemed like years, his mother saw listed the name of Vicente López. Could this be her son? She immediately followed up and found that this Vicente had been placed in a Mendoza orphanage. With the address written down and tucked safely into her purse, she boarded a bus for the hour-and-a-half trip to Mendoza.

A taxi took her to the orphanage. There, she learned that the boy, if he was her son, was about to be adopted. He had already spent a weekend with his new family. When she asked for more information, she was surprised to hear that the date and time for signing the adoption papers was that very day!

Exasperated, the mother asked, "Where is he now?"

A staff member quickly transported her to the court house, where she easily found the chamber where the ceremony was taking place. She opened the door and saw her son—or so she thought. He faced away from her, standing among some adults.

"Vicente?" she shouted.

Everyone turned to see the source of the question as she rushed toward them, but it was Vicente who answered.

"Mama!" he yelled, and he rushed into her arms.

They would never be parted again. Still, Vicente could not forget the couple who had almost adopted him.

◊ ◊ ◊

Then came a pause, as if the story had ended. But the voice, as was its owner's want, bellowed, *"Bueno, continua. ¡Hay más!* Well, go on. There is more!"

*"Bueno.* Vicente grew into a relatively handsome man."

*"¡Espera! ¿Qué dice?* Wait! What did you say?"

"Okay, a handsome man."

Vicente fell in love with and married Celia Camporo. He became an electrician working in a large bank building, and she taught primary school. They gave birth to and raised three daughters, one who went to Europe where she received a Doctorate of Philosophy and taught Honors courses at a major university in the United States. Her two sisters both went to college, one becoming a phycologist and the other, like her mother, a primary school teacher.

Vicente danced Tango, loved music of all kinds—especially the folk music of the local Peñas, a get-together with an open stage. He recited poetry from memory, read the daily newspaper, and religiously watched the news on television. He and his family lived in a modest house with a garage that Vicente converted into a work shed. He created a patio replete with an *horno* and permanent barbeque. And, he became famous for his asados, including his recipe for *pollo injectado*. Instead of barbecuing chicken with the sauce on the outside, Vicente developed a whiskey and lemon-based concoction that he injected into the chicken before putting it on the grill. His culinary fame spread enough that when a papal legation came to town, he was asked to do the barbeque for the special dinner for nearly a hundred guests.

When his daughters were little, the oldest around seven years old, he loaded the family in their car and drove to Mendoza. Vicente wanted to thank his almost adopted parents and share with them what had become of him. He wanted them to see that now he had a family. They had a happy reunion over food and wine. They traded their respective memories of that long-ago time and, then, what became of them.

Years after that, Vicente went to a pharmacy to pick up some medicine. As usual, Vicente had to wait with other customers. Then, the pharmacist called out his name. Just as he rose from his seat, a man rushed up to him.

"Vicente López! Vicente López! I know you. You knew my brother, Rafael Sosa. He was in the orphanage with you. He went with you to Mendoza. What happened to him? I have been looking for years. Do you know anything about him?"

Vicente's answer was a disappointment to him and the man. He explained how he and Rafael were recruited to look for bodies and then transported to Mendoza. The boy was still at the orphanage when Vicente and his mother were reunited.

He could only whisper, "No, friend. I never went back to the orphanage. I never saw him again. I don't know. He survived the quake. Probably he was adopted. I am sorry, but I can't tell you anything more."

◊ ◊ ◊

"There, Grand Jefe. There is your story. The first time I met you was in the patio of your house. You organized an asado for the extended family and friends. With the meat done, you sat at the end of a long table. The family buzzed around you as they took their seats. Your wine glass was filled merely by the wave of a finger. There was no question who the family patriarch was. And you welcomed me and we became friends when I answered a request from you with, '*Sí, mi jefe! Como me mande.* Yes, my boss! At your command!' From that afternoon, you became *El Gran Jefe* and you referred to me as *El Jefe*. It was our joke and mutual admiration."

"You were the master of the open-fire grill, which, in Argentina, is saying something. Once the meat was over the coals, you taught me that the two most important things for a good outcome was low heat and patience."

"And you and Celia travelled to the United States to visit your oldest daughter. Celia had suffered a stroke and was sick. But you went anyway. You picked weeds in your daughter's garden, happy for the solitude and to help."

"You are worthy of admiration and more. Your spirit cannot be forgotten. You live in my memory and in the lives of your daughters, two of whom published books, one of which contains a short story about you."

"Your life is the extreme opposite of a man born in riches. You were left in an orphanage, alone during the devastation of an earthquake, and found again by your mother. From childhood you grew to immortality in spirit and memory. How you suffered the death of Celia! You kept her framed photograph and would not forget her. You lived beyond the physical deaths. Your daughters buried both of your ashes under a tree, giving it the same nourishment that your spirits give us."

"And that is the point, *verdad?*"

"*Sí, y buena escuchar.* Yes, and good to hear."

# Fate VIII

THE SPIRIT SPOKE. "You asked if there is a God. My answer is that it is a matter of faith. Yes, faith. And you are a doubter—why not? You are also reasonable. In a logical way. You understand that between faith and reason, there is very little in common."

"Of course. 'Blind faith' speaks to that tension. I understand."

"But there are commonalities and places—frontiers you might say—where the two meet, even overlap."

"So, now you will tell me there is a God."

"No. That is up to you. Your paradigm. Imagine that God appeared to you. You are confronted with the image, the description of which does not matter. The image of a celestial something, even with an aura, which, incidentally, all physical human beings have—but the knowledge and sight of them have faded in time."

"I have an aura?"

"Yes, and it's fairly brilliant. A good thing. But we are straying from the point. So, God is before you and expresses his desire that he will endow you with celestial powers because he sees in you the humanity he seeks for all humankind."

"Wow! I would question his or her judgment."

"No. You would question your sanity: 'Is this real? Is this an illusion?' You would doubt what you see and hear, but you know you are present and awake, or so you feel."

"So, where, what—like now?"

"God steps off of a four-story roof and invites you to join him. Do you go?"

"If God invites me, of course."

"That is not what will happen. Your reason will interfere. Your sense of the reality of the situation will prevail, and you will imagine stepping into air and falling to your death. You even imagine the comments about your death. Obviously, people will say that you committed suicide, and your friends and family had no idea you were so depressed. So, you hesitate and do not follow. Reason triumphs over faith."

"But that is not true of everyone. There are some who would take the step, that 'leap of faith.'"

"We are talking about you, but, yes, some would acquiesce. People do not always deal with rational emotions. Feelings spring from the depth of one's entails—their spirit or subconscious. However, if, in the same scenario, God asked you to walk on water, would you go? Of course, you would. Why? Because you can swim; the request is not life threatening. Your logic and faith have come to a common place. And, by the way, even more people would take that step."

"Actually, that is a very logical scenario. Faith is not the priority. Logic, maybe pride of life, matters more than faith. And if that is the case overall, what value is there to faith?"

"Oh, don't get yourself depressed. You have faith in many things and those many things may add up to the celestial something that can be God. That is for you, actually us, to contemplate."

"Well, then. Are there dogs in heaven?"

"Not a trivial question, actually. Again, a matter of faith. In return for that question, I have one for you: Is the Disney character Goofy a dog or a cow?"

"I often thought about that and decided it depends on the point of view. Or, perhaps, the obvious answer is, 'only God knows.'"

"It's a matter of faith because reason does not apply here."

"And morality? Where is morality in all this? There are people who refute morality altogether. Tell me, is morality a concept that is real?"

"So, we have come to this: Imagine a place, concept, world, whatever, without morality. What is morality?"

"To know right from wrong."

"The very basic definition. In other words, most people know how to act, that there are limits."

"Yes, the legal standard that you cannot yell 'fire' in a crowded theater and create panic."

"For any reason, short of there being an actual fire."

"So, morality is real."

"If there is, in fact, a fire. Otherwise, every reasonable person would say so. But your question arises from a concern that today's world has given rise to alternative realities, that what you see may not be true. Or, it is possible to create new realities that are not in fact based in truth."

The spirit paused for a reaction.

"Yes. Everything is a performance. Hitler created his great parades, killed millions, destroyed cities to make his point. He created a new reality."

"Surprise, huh? Narcissism is based on an alternative reality that is true only in the depths of that sickness and those who would believe the narcissist. Look at some of your own politicians, much less some of the sorry examples that history provides us."

"The 'disappeared' in Argentina. What Putin's Russia has done to Ukraine. The idea that the only good Indian is a dead Indian. Human slaughter in southeast Asia or Middle East conflicts. These examples are not good indicators of what we humans are."

"No. On its face, no. But listen, all the people involved in those examples have no moral compass. A moral person would not order the deaths of his political enemies by throwing them out of planes into the ocean, or marching people of a different religion into gas chambers, or arbitrarily destroying cities for geographical gain with no thought that these are human beings who have died to satisfy an ego or a government."

"I totally agree."

"Of course, you do. If you did not, this conversation would not occur."

"But, you know, there are those today, youth, who believe in alternative reality. Especially in the arts."

"Yes. This is not new. We already discussed surrealism."

"Well, yes, but technology has advanced the idea to where propaganda—"

"And these folk do not want to hear about morality because they believe their art has no limits. Am I correct?"

"Exactly what I was thinking."

"Of course."

"I have heard it said that they would even be audacious enough to use the Inquisition as a form of art in that the burnings were staged for an audience."

"Not unlike the examples we just talked about. So, what is missing? The morality of staging such an event?"

"I would argue no. I know that a lack of morality had something to do with those examples. I would argue that there are limits, moral limits, right and wrong limits, to what we as humans do."

"But sometimes those immoral people, as you would call them, believe they are doing the moral thing."

"Even so, it does not justify what they are doing. Even during the times of the Inquisition, people knew it was wrong. Some of Hitler's own advisors tried to stop him. In my own country, there were always people who knew that slavery was wrong, morally wrong."

"And?"

"And, over time, we have learned that what might have been accepted before cannot be accepted now."

"So time discovers truth. What is right or wrong evolves."

"I suppose. But I worry when I hear some today argue that morality is not a concept, and reality or truth do not exist. I reject Pessoa's argument that we do not exist. That reality can be turned on its head so that there is no reality."

"And that worries you."

"With no morality, what is left but chaos? Although, no technological gimmick, an artist's magic can get away from two truths."

"Go ahead. I know what you will say."

"Man is nothing but a shit-making machine and death is the real reality. When the advocates of alternative reality can change those two things, I will be convinced. Until then, we all would be better off to give a knowing nod to them and continue in the real world, guided by our moral compass with some concept of right and wrong."

# Relevance
## (Mary Nordal)

IN A SMALL HOUSE ON AN INDISCREET STREET in the Los Angeles suburb of El Sereno, an elderly lady, perhaps in her sixties—but she could have been older or, most likely, a little younger—lived with her violin-playing husband, Marty. Together they formed a small musical group with a couple of other friends. Mary had a nice voice, so she sang. Their music, one supposes, was nothing special—that is, unless you considered their audiences. They performed in a club attended by people their age and older. People who came together to reminisce, sip gin, and dance while holding each other.

Mary and Marty had additional incomes, for they owned the two properties and small houses on either side of their house. The rent supplemented their pensions. As such, they lived a quiet existence and were barely noticed by their neighbors. That is, with two exceptions.

A family with four children purchased a house two houses up the street from them. The oldest of this lot were two boys, then five and four years old. They discovered Mary, or maybe it was the other way around. The boys saw in her an older woman who was tall, but she really wasn't. And she was well-proportioned, although the youths perceived her simply as big. Mary loved to bake, especially cakes to share with the audiences who came to hear her sing. Many of them were very familiar and a majority were on a first name basis. It must have been her cooking, the smell of which meandered out her small kitchen window, that caught the attention of the two boys, who being somewhat responsible, were allowed to wander a little.

Mary's natural disposition drew her attention to, and quickly grew into, her affection for the two lads. She put down her spoons and opened the kitchen door next to her counter. Upon questioning the young tikes, she learned their names and were they belonged. She immediately walked them back to their house, where she met and then befriended the parents. Ever after, the boys were allowed to visit Mary. They never missed a baking session, which happened often. They watched with fascination as well as anticipation as Mary, always in her pointed, fur-lined, leather slippers, worked her kitchen magic.

She let them lick the residue frosting off the spoons and bowls. The bowl, of course, was the prize and Mary would announce, "Whose turn is it for the bowl?"

She knew the answer but always enjoyed the children's pleas and excuses.

Mary always resolved any minor debate to everyone's satisfaction, handing the bowl to one of the boys while reminding them that another one would be available tomorrow.

Because of her love for the two boys, Mary and Marty became friends with the whole family, even loaning them their car when the mother became pregnant with a fifth child and needed to go to the hospital. The father did a little handiwork for them. Marty offered to pay him for this work, but, at the father's suggestion, he agreed to give the oldest boy violin lessons. But those failed because, as Marty explained, the boy is lefthanded. And although they were much younger, the parents even went to the old-age club a few times to listen to Mary and Marty perform.

Mary talked with the boys. The subjects ranged from their favorite colors to the possums that inhabited their houses' overgrown backyards that extended down to a running creek with crawdads.

Mary said she liked the color green: "It is pretty and symbolizes life, like an evergreen tree. Our plants are green, and a green forest is the best. It is the color of hope. Do you think that is why we have Christmas trees?"

The boys immediately went through a litany of colors that they liked, but, in the end, they could not, nor would not, disagree with Mary. They, too, pronounced green to be their favorite color. And Mary's and Marty's Christmas tree radiated with little shimmering lights. Mary had that effect—her goodness radiated over the boys.

Eventually, Mary invited the boys in her living room to sit quietly and watch rehearsals of their small musical group. The boys sat is awe of the sounds produced by instruments as they harmonized together. Mary's voice impressed them, not so much that they questioned whether she was talented or not, but because they had not seen that part of her. The rehearsals became as desirable as the baking sessions.

This relationship continued for the next six or seven years. But, then, the rehearsals stopped. The two boys hardly noticed because the baking continued, until that too became rare and then stopped. The boys did not understand and asked their father about it. He explained that Mary had become sick.

The boys noticed that every so often an ambulance parked in front of Mary and Marty's house. They watched white-suited men take tanks into the house and bring others out.

Then, one day, the oldest boy, now eleven years old, was riding his bicycle on the sidewalk in front of the house when two of the ambulance men came out.

He asked them, "How is she doing? Is she well?"

One of the men looked at the boy and then at the other man. He smiled, or maybe snickered, and said, "She is much better today."

In fact, Mary Nordal had died. That is what he really meant; her suffering was over. But he could not have answered a kid's innocent question this way. She no longer suffered from the cancer that had infested her body.

Mary's funeral and burial took place at the famous Forest Lawn Cemetery in Los Angeles. The two boys with their father attended the funeral. It would be the first of many funerals in these kids' lifetimes, and it would be the first of many lifeless bodies they would see in open coffins. The father thought it important for them to be there for many reasons, not the least of which was her love for them. Their attendance was the least they could do in return.

Even more so, they both lived long lives and never forgot the few years they spent with Mary Nordal. And a bowl with leftover frosting will always remind them of her.

## Fate's Conclusion

AN ENSUING SILENCE INDICATED that the story had ended.

So he spoke: "Oh yes, I remember her. I even imagined her looking over me after she died."

"Of course you did. If you did not, how could I share this story with you? You see, she is buried in a cemetery among movie stars, war heroes, and politicians. The place actually organizes public tours. But none of them stop at Mary's grave or, for that matter, Marty's, who is with her. But she touched you and lives in you."

"Yes, I know. And if I went back to that cemetery, I would look for Mary's grave. I wouldn't bother with the others. Maybe Walt Disney's."

"Exactly my point. She was a good person, like the Grand Jefe. In fact, in your case, she was a perfect person. Yet she did not win wars or appear on television or in movies. Mary and Marty never recorded a record. All that she did was bring a little happiness to a few peoples' lives, including yours and your brother's."

"And, I am sure, my parents' lives."

"You can depend on it. So, you see, she was relevant—very much so, to you."

The sound of a slight breeze prompted the two speakers to pause.

Then, he said, "I wish. I wish I could tell her."

"Oh, you are and will."

"How?"

"Wait and see."

"I—I don't know what to think. If I am dead, how is it that I can think? Or, am I going nuts? This can't be a dream."

"It could be a daydream. You have done that many times and some of what you have heard here has come from that form of subconscious expression."

"That I have heard? No, you and the other voice, the images have—"

"Revealed we are you. We are your subconscious, your spirit. All of us are personifications of others, persons and things, concepts that resonated in you. Death is a part of life. So, too, is life a part of death. We welcome this moment. We—you—needed this moment. All of us are embedded in you. You, in effect, have been talking to yourself, having an inner conversation."

"I *am* nuts."

"Hardly. A mind is a wonderful thing. All these stories are yours. You stored them. The spirit and memories came from elsewhere and you, your curiosity, accepted them. Levigolde spoke to you through the reality of Raedwald's burial. You never met him, yet here he is, no doubt a personification of many of the people who lived during Raedwald's reign."

A vision of a medieval warrior in a golden helmet appeared as if in a fog and spoke: "We never met, yet you thought about me, a product of archaeological surmises that inspired a book, then a movie, and now you. It is a story I want to share, and your curiosity has fulfilled that desire. You reached into time and I came to you."

Two women appeared, holding hands. The first, young and dressed in armor, knowingly nodded.

"I suffered a horrible death after a short life," she said.

The second, an old lady and dressed like a queen, looked at the first and said, "And I suffered a long miserable life."

A man, dressed in a white balloon shirt with ties and a long face heightened by a pointed goatee, slowly walked out of some mist to stand with the two women. He held a quill in his right hand. In a very upright and formal manner, he stated, "And I, imprisoned twice, wounded in battle, died a pauper."

As he slowly and elegantly gestured toward the two women, he added, "But our memories live in people like you. Our lives continue to have value."

He turned to leave alongside the two women, but he hesitated and then turned back.

"I am personally pleased that you modeled one of your books after my Quixote," he added, and then he disappeared after the women.

The vision was replaced with another, this time a tall man dressed in overalls and a plaid shirt.

Ralph spoke: "My story would have been lost had it not been for my grandson who shared the memory of my plight. How many times? You were inspired. It was not easy. You heard it more than once. At times you even asked him to repeat it. And now—well, now, the spirit of my memory will be known to more than my grandson's audiences and well beyond his own life span."

Ralph faded to be replaced by a squat, bearded stranger dressed in a high collar, a three-quarter length coat over a black waistcoat, and breeches with odd-looking, three-quarter high shoes. The man spoke slowly with a British accent.

"And you, my dear man, were good enough, indeed, to take my Sherlock Holmes character, a personage who spoke to me often. I am indebted to you and pleased to have shared him with you in a way that even I had not foreseen. My creation has lived on."

He, too, faded only to be replaced. This time, a broad-shouldered, above-medium height man with a long face, blue eyes, thick lips, and receding hairline appeared.

"Tommy, you will remember. It was I who first told you about my uncle in the Civil War. A hero."

I could not help myself: "Grandpa!"

"Yes, and you laughed, but it sparked something in your mind. No, in the minds of my son and you. The two of you came together to revive my uncle's death. Sylvester's memory almost became forgotten. Only talk in the family saved it. But no longer is it a legend, but history."

"And his spirit?"

A soldier in blue answered, "I am in you as we all are."

"But you are here, there talking to me."

"We are in your subconscious."

"Mine? What, where is it?"

"You have been told. In you. This respite, a coma, or, in normal parlance, a near-death experience, has freed your imagination to let your spirits speak."

"To do what?"

"Reveal yourself."

"They are right." A woman appeared. She was not much older than fifty, wearing an apron over a cotton dress and in pointed leather slippers. "Your love of me— well, that has carried forth. Through the years, you can share it as I shared with you any leftover frosting."

Mary was replaced with the image of Vicente, dressed in shorts and a dirty shirt, holding a barbeque tool. "*Estamos juntos. Nosotros en San Juan y los otros. Todo en la mentalidad. ¿Puede imaginarlo, Jefe?* We are united. All of us in San Juan and the others. All in your mentality. Can you imagine it, Boss?"

"But wait…."

Too late. The void was again filled with a voice familiar to him, but he saw nothing.

"All of what you have seen and heard is in you. At this moment we are you—and others as well. The stories, memories have become part of your conscience. They are in your mind, and you, or your spirit, will express yourself in your writing."

Another voice spoke: "Yes! Marilyn is right! In writing. You are a historian. You have published books. Your curiosity, your imagination, your spirit has left you no choice but to share our stories, stories you have stored."

Marilyn added, "We live in you as more than a memory. We know that you strive to honor our memory. You have talked to us, whether you recognize it or not. Feelings such as love and hate, and everything in between, resonate beyond your physical being. They, too, become the legacies of each of us."

He spoke, "But have I pleased you?"

"Our answer would be nonsensible. It would be like praising yourself. However, the true answer lies in the deep recesses of your conscience."

Then came the voice he had heard first.

"Now is the time. You will waken from this near-death experience, but you will not forget it. Nor will we leave you. We are your conscience and spirit. We are you. Now you have the answer to death, life, memory, and, indeed, in some sense, infinity. You have a second lease on life. In fact, every day is a new lease on life. Why not end it now? Because you have more to give."

◊ ◊ ◊

He opened his eyes to find himself in bed with no one around. It was daylight. He felt ecstatic, even transported, possibly enchanted because he had a new lease on life, which, after all, is eternal. He pinched himself and, with a sense of recognition, he rose from his bed, went to his desk, and started to write notes.

I asked her what it was like to be dead.

"Well, right now," she said, "I'm *not* dead. But when I am, it's like … I don't know, I guess it's like being inside a book that nobody's reading."

*–Tim O'Brien,*
*U.S. American novelist,*
The Things They Carried

**—fin—**

ALL BOOKS ARE AN AMALGAMATION of the authors' experience and, in fiction at least, their imagination. Moreover, every author writes to make a point, no matter how subtle. This book is obvious on both scores.

The most obvious acknowledgment must go to the protagonists in the preceding pages, the majority of which are based on real, historical figures.

Special recognition must go to Allen Sprowl and John Reeder: the former, an uncle who listened to his father; and the latter, a good friend who did likewise with his grandfather. Their stories inspired me to write them, which resulted in this book.

Special thanks goes to Dr. Leslie Donavan, a professor who teaches in the University of New Mexico's Honors College. She heard about and then read the manuscript. Her reaction was to immediately recommend it to Casa Urraca Press. She never doubted its value.

Zach Hively, the editor at Casa Urraca Press in Abiquiú, New Mexico, accepted the manuscript without hesitation. Above all, he must be acknowledged for his willingness to publish books that don't fit the standard requirements or expectations of most other presses. Moreover, his professionalism is deeply appreciated.

I feel that this book and Casa Urraca Press were fated to come together, which, of course, is a continuation of the narrative.

*Thomas E. Chávez*
*Albuquerque, New Mexico*

THOMAS E. CHÁVEZ is a member of Spain's Royal Academy of History and the Historical Society of New Mexico. He is the former director of the Palace of the Governors in Santa Fe and the National Hispanic Cultural Center in Albuquerque. He has received the National History Medal from the Daughters of the American Revolution and the Zia Award from the University of New Mexico Alumni Association, at which university he earned his Ph.D. in history. He is the author of fourteen books to date, and he travels widely to give lectures and presentations. Chávez was born in New Mexico, where he continues to live.

www.ingramcontent.com/pod-product-compliance
Lightning Source LLC
Chambersburg PA
CBHW021716190726
48289CB00008B/2563